Peter in Flight

By Paul Michael Peters

ISBN:098917851X
EAN: 9780989178518

Cover Art By: Nicole Ray www.nicoleray.com

- for Cac

Chapter 1

Over the last six years I have shaken the hands of over a million people. After all, this simple act is the beginning of every business deal, providing the potential customer with his first and often lasting impression.

The worst handshake—number 4,528—was at the Marriott Copley Place in Boston, a hotel connected to a shopping center by a series of elevated walkways between high rises. I was at my booth in the Marriott's exhibit hall, by the entrance (a professional trade show guy takes pride in getting the best booth placement). I had a clear line of vision to the mall.

Business on the floor was slow, and one of the attendees had decided to skip the session altogether. She had made her way to the confectionary stand just outside the exhibit hall's door. She was tall and lanky, her black hair streaked with gray, and her belly protruded slightly; she looked more unkempt than unfit.

I can see the little drama play out in my mind as if it were happening now. She buys a half-pound of salt-water taffy, each piece wrapped in white wax paper, and the merchant puts them in a small brown paper bag. She turns and saunters back through the front door of the exhibit hall, taking a piece of taffy and shoving it into her mouth. Her chipmunk cheeks are stretched full of candy as she proceeds to walk in my direction.

I pretend I'm busy at the booth, but I'm fully aware of her every step. When she gets close enough for me to command her attention, I put my eager hand out, look her in the eye, and say, "Hello, I'm Peter. Can I tell you about my enterprise solution?"

That's when I know that things have gone wrong. I've acted too soon; I haven't read the situation correctly. Her hand moves to her mouth and she spits the well-chewed blue taffy onto her palm and hastily drops it into the brown paper bag for safekeeping. Without wiping her hand, she grasps mine firmly. My eyes are locked on hers. My fake smile is all a gleam. I must now ignore what has just taken place, and tell her all about my software to see if there's any opportunity of a sale.

My mistake? I didn't mirror the prospect. I should have let her lead me; I shouldn't have acted first. That was my rookie mistake in the spring of 1996.

Needless to say, she didn't buy the software. The company she represented didn't even fit our customer profile, being far too small. She was kind enough to stand at my booth and watch a product demonstration for ten minutes before saying "No, thank you," and walking away, leaving me with nothing but sticky hand. As she left, she reached into her brown paper bag to retrieve her half-chewed morsel.

As "the trade show guy," I can tell you that my story is about one thing: developing the expertise to find the people who will buy my software on trade show floors across North America. Last year, like the four before it, I spent forty-nine weeks on the road going from one event to the next. People go to conventions, and then they browse the trade floor, which is where I shine.

I do not own a home or a car. I do not have a family. I do not have an apartment. If we met on an airplane, in a hotel lobby, or on a conference floor, I would consider us to be friends. I might not remember your name without a name badge, but I will remember your story.

Peter in Flight

If you're considering this line of work, you should know that what I do has a rhythm that's pretty easy to understand. Most big trade shows set up on a Saturday or Sunday and last until Thursday of the following week. So on a Sunday I take about thirty minutes to set up my retractable booth on the exhibit floor. I check my list of items for each event, which always includes the prize drawing, entry cards, several staplers, company logo pens, electricity, and a monitor for the software demonstration. Once that's in place I make sure that the people from my company supporting the event have all checked into their hotel rooms and have their registration badges. Then I check my email. My Inbox is always full of messages: Someone missed his flight; someone can't find the hotel, someone can't locate the booth or wants to meet for dinner, or tells me there's been a software update to the product.

Each Monday morning I make a call to Kurt, a man I trust with my life and the head of my exhibit house—the place that creates the booth in which I'll live for the next four days. He and his team know every labor manager in every major city. When I mention the name of my exhibit house, things just seem to happen. Any success I might have in life is tied to knowing him and having him on my side.

An exhibit house is basically Santa's workshop for trade shows and exhibits. It's a magical place where they make things happen—they create specialized exhibits as well as store and ship exhibits. The front office has graphic designers, architects, and logistics experts. Dreams are realized here with paint, planning, and a few nails. In the adjacent building is a humidity- and temperature-controlled storage facility where all the exhibits not in use dream of the next big event.

Kurt happens to work at the most well-known of these businesses, one with two locations—one in Las Vegas (LAS) and the other adjacent to O'Hare (ORD). Kurt works in Chicago.

Our Monday morning call will go something like this.

"How's the road treating you this week?" Kurt will ask.

"There is no life better," I'll respond.

"I see you're in MCO this week and LAS next." He always uses airport codes. "Orange County is doing a dock cleaning this week with the Fire Marshal, so we're going to store property number 2 off-site."

MCO is the code for Orlando, Florida, and Kurt's referring to the Orange County Convention Center. In the real heat of central Florida, the empty cases and boxes we litter the place with could be a fire hazard, so the local official will do a walk-through to make sure things are safe. This is preceded by a courtesy call letting the convention center know he's coming out—hence, Kurt knows he's planning a visit. My "property" is the booth. In this case, booth number 2.

I have five properties that rotate with me depending on the size of the event and where I am. Three of the booths are the standard 10x10 and two are table-tops—small displays that fit on top of any standard hotel table. The three 10x10s can be reconfigured into one big booth when needed for those really big shows. The table-tops will join me at any event with two hundred registrants or less.

After Kurt and I are done with our Monday call, I speak with my boss Tatiana. Hers is the best handshake I've ever shared. She is my number one.

During my first phone interview, we just clicked. She was firm but fair, our language was similar, her voice melodious. Of course I was happy to meet with her. The first thing I noticed were her green eyes, soft and inviting. Her skin was pale and youthful, her hair dark, straight, and cut above the shoulder, and, in a certain light, brown highlights could be seen. Her lips were thin and provided a perfect balance to high cheek bones and the line of her chin. However, these were not what won me over. When we shook hands, there was a spark. I've tried to explain it as a static shock from the dry air and new carpeting, but who really knows the truth? Her fragrance filled my head like an intoxicating potion that sweetly burned my tongue on its way to my heart. My first thoughts on meeting her were "What am I in for?" I don't remember a thing about the interview outside of her. Yet, she still hired me.

Peter in Flight

Two weeks later I was going through orientation and found that my desk was located just outside her office. Each time she passed I was distracted by that tantalizing fragrance. From eight feet away I could hear the slippery fabric of her clothes move or the click of her nails on each key. On the days she wore a dress, I was lost knowing her youth had been spent perfecting ballet moves at the barre in front of a mirror.

There were, of course, barriers to our relationship. She was my boss, and thus I just couldn't find a way to express my burning desire to be with her. When something went wrong, I couldn't take her in my arms and tell her things would get better. Oh, and there was the small fact that she was married to this great guy and had two girls.

When I discovered that she was married with children, I fell into a funk. There was the week I stayed in bed and dropped a few pounds unintentionally. There were several days when I forgot to shave, sometimes shower. It was not the best of times.

It might have been fate that stepped in at that point. The woman who'd been handling the trade shows decided she no longer wanted to do them. When she gave notice, I jumped at the opportunity and in three months expanded the position to what it is today. It only took a single spreadsheet to prove that putting someone—me—on the road full-time could create a huge number of new named contacts for sales and elevate our company status.

My Monday calls with Tatiana often take a full hour, sometimes more. I look forward to this call each week. We talk about the office gossip, her life, her family, and eventually the marketing calendar. I'm always planning three months ahead of the current date, sometimes more. There are enough trade shows, conferences, breakfast briefings, road shows, and the annual users conferences in the software industry these days that I cannot attend them all in fifty-two weeks. Sometimes I need to double or triple up.

During the regular week I'm in the exhibit hall, shaking hands, demonstrating our product, promising a better life once they buy our software. In downtime, I'm filling out paperwork for an event later in the year or sending an email to staff about the schedule or hotel. Without the distractions of working from an office, I'd say I'm much more efficient as an employee than others. Yes, there are also times when I'm poolside, at the evening entertainment, or taking clients out to dinner and drinks, but those are also part of the job. How much fun it can be to spend three evenings a week with total strangers and their odd habits over dinner, listening to their problems and explaining how my company will solve them.

Some weeks I find myself at two to three smaller conferences rather than one large one. The table-top displays are set up in ten minutes, and while there are fewer hands to shake, there's just as much potential to sell. Combined smaller events make up most of my year and provide a higher quality of return to my software company.

I like to believe that Tatiana is concerned about me—that she worries about my well being and may even think about me after hours. There might be these moments, just after the lights go off, late at night when the kids are asleep and she's in bed with her husband, that she mentions me. "I'm worried about Peter," she might say. Often at this point in my fantasy the turbulence in the plane rumbles me awake or the early morning complimentary paper delivery to my hotel door will stir me back to reality. I am alone in the world. Just like many of you, I am my only savior, my only hero. Love is a luxury I cannot afford.

Chapter 2

Enterprise software, the line of product for which I am Comp-U-Soft's ambassador, is a combination of database management, calculations, and reporting. There are eighty-four companies that I compete with. Each of them, in one way or another, fills the needs of growing organizations with disparate data systems. As companies grow, many come to realize that they have picked up multiple software systems that make the organization run. Finance has one system, HR has another, and sales has a third.

Enterprise software offers the ability to take these separate departmental systems and tie them together. How? Well, they add a single database that several of them feed into. This central source of data allows executive and management teams to gather comprehensive information and run executive summaries. Some of these systems will roll the application out to lower levels of users to add data into the system. It's where calculations can be made, business forecasts built, and reports can be sent to the Security and Exchange Commission (SEC).

Hence, I can say to people at my booth, "Our software helps you bridge the business gaps you are currently experiencing." I can show them my cool reporting tool and ask, "Wouldn't you like to know if this sort of thing is happening in your company?" Certain types of reports can really seduce a CFO or CEO. They want to be able to drive the business as if it were a car, so these reports are called a dashboard. You can tell when things are heating up, going fast, moving slow, or have come to a complete stop. It also lets you see the road ahead with predictive analytics. For example, if I am at point A, and I do this, I can get to points B and C. But if this were to happen (God forbid) I would be a point J or K.

I can't speak for how well the software works, but I know how I work. Two things make me great at what I do. The first is sleep. I can sleep anywhere. Many people find it difficult to get comfortable in a strange or new place. For the most part I find myself in some of the higher-end hotel chains. Event organizers are catering to senior level executives with higher standards. They can afford the two- hundred-fifty dollar room that lower level employees wouldn't have the budget for.

Sleep is an important part of what I do. You'll need to be at your best as an ambassador for your company, and that includes a keen mind. You can't get good sleep if you are drunk. Alcohol, while widely glamorized as the magic elixir producing a signed agreement, is often the downfall of successful event marketers. You can decide to drink, or you can stay up late, but you cannot both stay up late and drink before your scheduled stint in the booth. Anyone naïve enough to believe that has been sent home early or lost an opportunity for the company.

The second thing that makes me great at my job is kindness. People just want to be treated well. Not better or differently, just treated well. My grandmother told me that the true sign of a gentleman is thinking of others before thinking of one's self. For some reason, I believed her. It's an idiom that has carried me through life. People want to be listened to, not just heard. Fortunate or not, I now know the stories of thousands of people who feel that they can open up to a stranger about the most personal of topics.

The confessions usually come at the end of a reception and start with the phrase "You seem like a pretty nice guy." Which is true. I *am* a nice guy. I may be the nicest guy in the world. On any flight, you can sit next to me and tell me your tales, and I will remember them. Last November, between San Diego and San Francisco, I had to help a gentleman in his late 60's who appeared to have slower cognitive skills zip his pants and buckle his belt after a visit to the rest room. I look at it as being part of the job.

The world in which I live, between the trade show floor and the airline seat, is filled with lonely business travelers. They're accustomed to a staff member, spouse, or friend wherever they go. They're looking for a buddy at the trade show, or a kind ear on a flight. What they usually get is pushing and shoving for carry-on luggage, delayed flights, overworked ticket agents, and unfamiliar territory. When they meet me, they have a friend and companion, even if only for a few short hours.

I awake early at the Grand Hyatt Atlanta in Buckhead. It's Tuesday. My day will start at the booth, shaking the hands of senior level executives while they drink coffee and eat pastries. Once they go into session I'll have two hours before they take a break.

During lunch I'll sit next to one of two people I've been keeping my eye on since we first met during the Sunday evening reception. One is a CFO, the other a controller. Both work for companies in my target audience, both have watched the product demonstration, and one of them is going to win our prize drawing, the newly-released portable DVD player by Panasonic. Everyone else is still giving away a digital camera and is about six months behind the curve of what I'm doing (a trade show guy takes pride in having a unique and interesting prize for each event).

I end up having lunch with the controller, which is fine with me. Other people will push to get to the top person and hope for a reference downward, a decent strategy when you can pull it off. But you still need to be able to start with the person who really runs things, and a controller is a better bet for that. The CFO might give you a list of twenty people who you then need to contact. If you get to the right one first and win them over, then maybe you've made a sale. On the other hand, the controller might be the right person straight off the bat.

Peter in Flight

After lunch there's another series of sessions and, when I check my voice mail, I find there's a message from Tatiana. Her voice is mellifluous and warms my heart as she tells me about one of our executives who's speaking next week at a conference. Even the most competent executive needs to be watched over. There are tasks that either evade or exceed their comprehension. The four emails I've sent him earlier are no longer at the top of his mailbox, so I'll send a new one for clarification.

Often, the senior executive develops a conflict in his schedule and can no longer be available to speak. I'm then called on to present on his behalf. So while I'm not a regular speaker on the circuit, roughly twice a month I present on a topic I know little about. The first time this happened I'm sure several people asked for a conference refund. By now I am one of the highest-scored speakers on evaluations.

Back in my room I connect to the telephone and hear the connection signal letting me know I can turn on my email. I hope for the day when this is a faster process as it only takes seconds for me to find the email in question and forward it.

There is also a note from Tatiana hoping I am well and safe, and reminding me to call her when I have the chance to talk about our user conference.

Aside from my duties as the ambassador of software, I am also responsible for the coordination of a third of the program at the annual Comp-U-Soft Users Conference. This is the 10th anniversary of bringing all of our customers to one location to feed them, educate them, and make them feel loyal, grateful, and beholden to us. We are only expecting six hundred people. Two years ago the board split off a segment of the product that specialized in retail software. This also reduced the number of customers by two-thirds.

Tatiana and I will arrive in Orlando on that Friday, and I look forward to our time together. In the afternoon, we'll meet with the hotel's convention planner and walk through the details of what they call a "BEO" (or banquet event order) as well as work out any last minute changes with vendors. This will be followed by dinner and conversation long into the night. Then back to reality in the morning when the other members of our team arrive for set-up and I have to share Tatiana with the rest of the world again.

Chapter 3

My 11:35 AM flight from ATL to SAN is on schedule. ATL, Atlanta's Hartsfield airport, is the largest and busiest in North America and competes annually with London's Heathrow for busiest in the world. SAN, or San Diego is mid-sized but not busy. It's a very relaxed and welcoming environment.

Atlanta is actually where things started for me. When I was eight, my mother was dating a man—a pretty good guy I guess—who also had a young son. The two of them loved Chex cereal. At the time Republic Airlines was running a promotion with Chex in which you could turn in box tops for a plane ticket.

Maybe he was thinking of asking my mother to marry him and wanted to see if the two of us would get along. Anyway he exchanged Chex box tops for a ticket to Atlanta where I joined him for a week. Sitting in the executive lounge, reflecting on this story, I have to say those were different times in America. No one in her right mind today would send her eight year old off on an airplane to spend a week in a hotel with a strange man. After his meetings, we'd get something to eat, climb Stone Mountain, see local attractions. Otherwise I sat in the hotel room. I'd planned to swim, but the staff wouldn't allow an unaccompanied child in the pool. Furthermore, the hotel was circled by a vast parking lot and back home I wasn't allowed to cross the street.

Turner Cable was pretty new at the time, so I ended up watching the James Bond movie "For Your Eyes Only," twice a day, every day that week. I still know the entire script by heart.

The girl in the seat next to me is blonde, in her earlier twenties, and excited. She smiles as she looks out the window at the luggage crew.

The plane fills and we get as comfortable as possible. Attendants are walking up and down the aisle with last minute pushes to overhead compartments or reminders to tighten our seatbelts.

She seems a bit worried when I look up from my book and smile.

"Hi, my name is Peter," I calmly say.

"I'm Megan."

"Is San Diego your final destination?"

"Yeah, my sister Annie is stationed there. She's in the Navy."

"That's great. When was the last time you got to see one another?"

"Christmas."

"And what do you do? Are you in the Navy?"

"No," she says as if I were silly to think it. "I work in a doctor's office."

And with this sentence, it begins. Her nerves evaporate; she's concentrating on the moment. I'm a nice guy who will listen, and she'd like to tell her story. Between Annie and herself, there's a middle sister, Danielle. She and Danielle share the same parents while Annie has a different father. The three of them were raised by different adults—Danielle was raised by their father, Megan by their grandmother, and Annie was raised by her mother.

Megan is a single mom who still dates her baby's father, a Filipino who wants them to live with his mother in the Philippine tradition of keeping a family together under one roof. She's been working at the doctor's office for about eight months now and has decided to go back to school so she can be a nurse. In fact, she's brought along some nursing books and wants to share them with me, which she does for a good hour. Unfortunately, she works for a gynecologist and the full color photos and diagrams, along with her narration, are much more than I am prepared to view on an airplane.

About an hour before the plane lands, Megan returns to the story of her life. In detail she tells me that her father was a bum who couldn't pay a bill on time. Once her mother died, it was a difficult choice to make, but she went with her grandmother while Danielle was independent enough to live with their father. Only in the last two years had the three sisters begun to grow closer, after the birth of Megan's son. Annie and Danielle wanted to be good aunts. The photos from her purse prove how great a kid he is.

After the plane lands, as I gather my things and make my way up the bridge to the gate, she calls for me to slow down. She explains that someone is going to meet her in baggage, but she needs to find the right carousel. I point my new friend in the proper direction, tell her to look for the signs, and politely say it's been a long trip and I need to wash my hands.

Eight minutes later when I emerge from the men's room she's standing like a lost puppy by a trash can just outside. "Where were you?" she scolds.

"I was in the men's room, like I said."

"Well let's go, I don't want to miss my ride."

"You're going to be okay."

I escort her to the baggage claim at the bottom of the escalator and help her grab her bags. We walk over to the circle where cars pick up passengers who have just arrived. Within seconds of stepping outside she becomes worried again; this new experience is more than she bargained for.

I write my cell number on the back of my business card and tell her, "Listen, your ride's going to be here. It's just going to take a second for you two to connect. But if you don't see your ride in an hour, just call my cell phone. I'll come get you; we'll figure this out. My hotel is five minutes away."

She seems relieved by this. Still, I stand with her to make certain she's going to be okay. After ten minutes, a very fit and confident woman calls Megan's name; it's Annie.

Megan acts as if she's been rescued from prison. "Annie, this is Peter. He was on the flight with me. Peter, this is my sister Annie."

"Hi, Peter," Annie says.

I shake hands with number 1,000,428. "Pleasure to meet you."

"Thanks for waiting with Megan; she can get turned around."

"My pleasure. I should thank Megan for keeping me company on that long flight." I turn to her. "I hope you complete school as you plan to."

"I will, Peter."

The two sisters, now reunited, hug and are off for their adventures. I am alone once more and get in the taxi line. Within minutes I'm at my hotel, checked in, unpacked, and ready for the next conference.

Chapter 4

So why would you want to talk to me rather than to the dozens, sometimes hundreds, of other exhibitors at a trade show or conference? It's true, my booth says the right things to grab your initial interest. But why stop and talk? Well, I'll tell you why. Because I speak to you as a human being first, not to your title or your job. Because I'm offering you the chance to "Enter to Win" with a tasteful sign at perfect eye level just at the edge of my space—a great new electronic device or another coveted object you can keep or present as a gift for a birthday or the holidays.

I budget each prize I give away at between $350 and $650 depending on the size and importance of the event. If I can get 200 to 500 names from the conference, it's more than worth it.

It took me six months to perfect the entry form. The basics are there—the same information that's on your business card: name, title, address, company, phone, fax, and email address. Right next to this in a faint gray but easy-to-read font it says, "Staple your business card here." I always have three or four small staplers on hand for entrants to use.

Below this, I ask for information about the entrant's business. I've provided boxes beside annual revenue ranges that are appealing to me.

I ask what system is currently being used, to allow a follow-up by the sales department. I'm interested in how eager the company is to adopt a new system. And finally, one simple and right to-the-point question, "Who is the best person to follow up with at your company?"

Too many questions and people are discouraged from filling out the form completely. Ask them, "May I follow up with you?" and they think you're going to harass them with endless phone calls. Leave off the part about stapling your business card and some just walk away. No, this is the perfectly-sized, designed, and shaped survey about who they are and what they need.

At the end of each night I return to my room to sort through this stack of entry forms. I can quick scan the checked boxes and find the right ones for follow up. If we've had a conversation in more detail, I've written notes on the back of the form. The good prospects go in one pile, the bad ones in another. Each of the good ones I type into a spreadsheet and send off to Tatiana for someone to enter into systems for follow-up from the telemarketing sales team.

Some sales people are hunters who track down target accounts; others are farmers who grow relationships until they are ready to harvest. I think of myself as a fisherman out on the seas of life, pulling in a large catch, and sorting through them all to throw back the small ones to grow bigger.

I'm in New York, at the Jacob K. Javits Convention Center this week for a large technology event with many of our partners in attendance. I'm here to support our two largest partners. Our booth is tiny in comparison to theirs, but we have an ideally located space on the end of an aisle where there is steady foot traffic as people walk the show floor, either through good fortune or my experience and skill.

By the end of the second day, the two women working the booth with me have made close connections with key members of our two primary partner groups. Each will be taking a partner to dinner that evening with members of their team to make sure they remember us when the key integration questions come up or marketing dollars for a joint campaign become available.

While they head out, I decide to walk from the convention center back to my hotel room in Times Square. Being outside for such a long walk feels good.

On my very first trip to Manhattan, years ago, I distinctly remember piles of blue trash bags lining each traffic-packed street. I asked my companion in the cab from LaGuardia if there was a garbage strike in the city. . He explained that New York was like this each evening, especially in the summer, a "hot smelly mess of humanity."

Each return to New York reminds me of that conversation. There are so many people in one place it's hard to comprehend. Comedian Dennis Miller used to say, "Even if I'm a one-in-a-million type of guy, there are 30 of me running around China." And that's the real challenge, isn't it?

When it comes to finding the right person in your life, a lot of choices are involved for both people; you need a system to filter out unlikely candidates. Is there an entry form I can create on which prospective partners can tick off the appropriate boxes so I can make certain they are the "right person"?

I stop by a corner deli for a sandwich before settling in for the night. Once all the important data is keyed into the spreadsheet, I shoot it off to Tatiana. Then I go through my email and review my travel and events for the rest of the month.

My cell phone chimes with the tone I've programmed that tells me it's Tatiana, and of course I pick it up.

"Hey, how are you?" I say happily.

"Good. I saw your spreadsheet and took a chance you were still working."

"You know me, always working."

"Looks like a good event."

"Yeah, I've been pretty happy with the conversations we've been having on the floor. Our partners are keen to do some programs with us this year. I told them you'd be the right person to follow up with."

"Good. Nice work. Any exciting stories from the road?"

"Getting a taxi out of LaGuardia was a hassle. There was a line that snaked through these yellow barriers like at an amusement park, with an airport tyrant at the end barking out orders. He was lining up taxis three wide to make things go faster, but blocking cabs behind them from passing. When people jumped in, it was a race to see who could get out of the loading area first."

"Sounds crazy."

"So I get in my cab, and the driver hits the gas, throwing me into my seat. This happens over and over, stop and start. Each light he hits is red and we wait. Once it turns green, it's a drag race."

"Sounds awful."

"Actually, this is normal. This is every trip from the airport to Manhattan I've ever taken."

"So what's different about this one?"

"We get to Grand Central Parkway to take us into the city, and it's gridlock. And I notice this smell."

"Oh no."

"I look to the driver's ID and you wouldn't believe his name."

"What? What is it?"

"Kong King." She laughs. "And Kong is obviously wearing a pair of adult diapers so he can work non-stop."

"No," she cries in disgust.

"All the windows are down and I'm stuck in traffic for who knows how long."

"What did you do?"

"What could I do? I opened a tin of mints and took a handful in my mouth, hoping to balance things out."

"It's been a few years since I had to change a diaper, and I've had some stinkers, but adult-sized.... Yuck." She laughs.

It's always good to hear her laugh. She has a great laugh that makes you want to try with all your might to keep it going.

"Yes, my job is so glamorous."

"Aw," she sympathizes, "you're doing such a great job. Don't let the world's smelliest taxi driver break your spirit."

"I won't."

"Hey, we're going to see each other soon, don't forget. I'm looking forward to hearing more stories of adventure and travel in Orlando, so save some good ones for me."

"I will. How are things with you?"

"Well," she says, "you know how things are in the office. Meetings, phone calls, planning, meetings about plans or phone calls. Jack had nice things to say about you picking up that presentation. The event organizers said you scored really high on the surveys."

"I just do what I can out here."

"You're too humble."

"Everything else okay?"

"I have some stories for you as well. You get to buy the first round."

"Sounds good." There's a pause, and in that silence I can't help myself from saying, "It's great to hear from you." I say it in the most sincere way I can without getting sappy.

"Yeah, I always enjoy our time on the phone together."

Even the silence is enjoyable for me, knowing she's on the other end of the line. In the background I can hear someone's voice and her hand covers the receiver. I hear her say dimly, "Just a minute, I'm on the phone for work."

Her voice becomes more official. "I have to go," she says, "but send me the final sheet when you can tomorrow. We want to get those into the system ASAP. Don't forget to mail the paper versions for backup. Call if you have any questions and I'll see you in Orlando in two weeks."

"Yes, of course. I appreciate you checking in. Good night."

"Good night," she says. And she's gone.

The next afternoon the event closes at the Javits Center and I pack the leftover materials to send on to Kurt. Kurt will keep the good literature and toss the dog-eared stuff, repack for the next show, and make it ready for distribution when I need it.

It's started to rain. The line for cabs is huge, but there isn't a single taxi in sight. Dragging my carry-on, I head up two blocks and over three, sprinting between building scaffoldings and awnings for the next dry spot. At the next corner a taxi has stopped to let a woman out, and I jump in. Before closing the door I hear the woman say with a snide remark, "Good luck with this one."

As the word "LaGuardia" leaves my lips, I'm thrown back into my seat. The driver is in a heated conversation on his cell phone and we quickly make our way across town to the FDR. Once we get on the blacktop that follows the East River, I find the strength to lean forward and see that we're going 75 as he swerves between cars. Near the waste building, he slows to 70 and jumps back to top speed once he makes it past another set of slower cabs.

Rolling up fast on the RFK Bridge, he takes the turn at full speed and picks an open lane approaching the toll booths. His E-Z Pass clicks off, and he lets go of the steering wheel to add the $3.50 toll to the black fare box mounted to the dashboard. His left knee is the only thing steering the cab as we hit the dip on the other side of the tolls and the car takes to the air. His right hand returns to the wheel over the bridge and onto the slick Grand Central Parkway. We are minutes from LGA at this point when the ringing of a second cellular phone starts to play a dance number. His right hand pats the pile of papers and empty fast food bags in the passenger seat until he discovers the device.

We roll up to the departures area at LGA under the power of his left knee and he stops both conversations to say, "$32.50."

I hand him $35 and he sets down one phone to take the money and hand me a receipt. As I get out, with my bag in hand and a thankful prayer for my life, a businesswoman becomes his new fare.

"Good luck with this one," I say, and she looks at me as if I'm the asshole before the cab peels out and disappears.

Peter in Flight

I head inside for check-in. Quickly I find the ticket kiosk and swipe my frequent flyer card. In less than a minute, out spits the ticket and I'm walking through the first-class metal detector, as I watch my computer bag and roller bags ride the conveyer belt. On the other side I walk to the small "executive lounge" I'm a member of to enjoy cranberry juice and pretzels while CNN repeats the stories of the day. Then I walk over to my gate for the next destination.

Chapter 5

Orlando is as it was when I left last month—hot, growing, and full of opportunity. It's a top-tier location for events, along with New York, Chicago, San Francisco, Atlanta and Phoenix. In each of these you can find major hotel accommodations suitable for any size event, an airport with several flights from around the globe daily, and a rich resource of entertainment options.

I arrive at the Marriott World Center in Orlando a day ahead of Tatiana in order to make the time adjustment from San Francisco a little easier. The Marriott is ideally situated for our event's attendees—only moments from the Walt Disney World Properties—with lots of rooms and large ballrooms. An added benefit is that the hotel has agreed not to sell the remaining space to another large event.

We'll own the space, so that everyone you meet in the elevator or in the hallway is your peer. Hotel staff are focused on our group alone. Tatiana is very good at planning. She's also very good at finding locations our customers enjoy.

There was a moment last year when we were doing a site inspection that I almost said something to her. I struggle with the knowledge that my feelings for her are merely a chemical reaction. Her pheromones are a high match for my receptors. It's biology, pure and simple. Nothing else makes sense of it. So I decided against it.

Nevertheless, although she's unavailable, uninterested, and off limits, no matter where I go, no matter how long it's been since I last saw her, she fills my thoughts. My better angels have always told me to think of her daughters first, her loving and fortunate husband next, and to know that, at best, I would only be a rude and misguided man who did not know his place in the world.

She arrives at the hotel on time that morning. I'd forgotten how lovely she always looks. She has thin lips always covered in lip gloss, one of those quirky attributes that are perfectly flawed and therefore even more attractive. Her smile takes over her face because of it, a great smile I'm happy to see again.

"Did you see the weather?" she asks.

"No," I lie. "I haven't checked."

"There's a huge hurricane just off the coast. It's moving our way."

"Well, that's not good."

"No, it's not. I got a call from the hotel and they're talking about evacuation plans. How did you not hear about this?"

"I haven't turned a television on in a few days."

"Let's get to this meeting and we can catch up. Are you all right? You look a little sad."

"Me? I'm great, happy to see you, ready for the big event."

"You'd tell me if something were up, wouldn't you?"

"Tatiana, I tell you everything. There are no secrets between us," I lie again.

The news is accurate. Tatiana was on one of the last flights landing at ORD that day. All in-coming flights are being rerouted. The hurricane is on its way. Even Disney, for the first time, will be closing the parks.

Fortunately the Marriott was a hurricane shelter for many years. Unfortunately, it lost its status last year with a change in the codes. We should be fine, but the conference is cancelled.

She and I go through the list of attendees and staff, calling each to explain the cancellation. I let her deal with the executive team while I call the vendors to see if they're going to charge us full price or if this act of God will kick in some triggers. Three hours later she turns to me and says, "I'm ready for a drink. Buy me a drink, Peter."

We find the hotel lobby empty and the bar and restaurant closed. Minimal staff is staying on-site for operations while the rest have gone home or have headed for higher ground.

Tatiana has the keys to the vacant presidential suite. The most senior of our staff were going to use this large room to host private meetings with customers over the next week. Now it's our secluded clubhouse to watch the impending storm move in from the coast. The large plasma televisions are each set to different news feeds with a scrolling red bar at the bottom. On the action map, a big purple swirl surrounded by orange, yellow and green outer bands is slowly moving in our direction. She's on her third mini-bottle of vodka and I on my second of gin. Her spirits are high when her cell phone rings. She flips it open to see it's her husband. While she walks to a separate room, I hear her say, "Hi, yeah I know it's on the way. No, I can't leave" before the door closes.

I can already sense that the alcohol was a poor choice. My guard is down and I'm suddenly more willing to take a chance on foolish things I know I shouldn't. Being drunk in an emergency also seems stupid. If asked to walk down the twenty-eight flights of stairs in the next five minutes, I know there's a growing possibility that I might stumble or fall.

In the next room is a beautiful woman I care very much about. In the next three hours a giant wall of water, wind, and debris will hammer at this building unrelentingly. If not now, when? If not her, then who?

"Hey," she says when she returns fifteen minutes later.

"Hey," I say.

"Any change?"

"It's slightly closer. Everything alright at home?"

"Yeah, he's worried. He's not sure what to do."

"There's nothing to do but wait. Sometimes waiting is the only thing you can do."

"That's what I told him. There's nothing to be done."

With a crack of the plastic seal, she's into the fourth mini-bottle and empties it into a glass with ice. I'm still working on mine when she sits down next to me on the couch. Her head is now on my shoulder. She makes herself comfortable.

"This is nice. Normally I'm covered in sticky children who want something from me. I've turned into a jungle gym for the girls to practice gymnastics or ballet on."

"Not to mention brushing hair."

"It's everywhere, all tangled and out of control, and with each stroke of the brush they scream."

"I can't imagine something more fun."

"Sometimes at home I just want to stop being touched."

"Time for yourself, I understand."

She finishes her drink and puts her glass on a coaster. "You seemed a little sad this morning. Is everything okay? You know you can't hide anything from me. I know you too well."

"When I was in St. Louis a few weeks ago at that little event we were testing out, a strange thing happened."

"What?"

"I checked into my hotel, got to my room, and the light was flashing on the phone. Most of these bigger chains have that automatic welcome message when you check in, so I didn't think much of it. But this was a small place, an old place right on the waterfront by the Arch. They didn't have this new message system. So I listen."

"And?"

"And it's this woman, calling her husband. She says 'Hi honey, I love you so much and miss you. The kids are great, we're all looking forward to seeing you tonight. I went to that little store and I'm wearing something new for tonight. I love you.' Then the message ends."

"That's funny," Tatiana said half-heartedly. "If she only knew that you got it instead of her husband."

"Yeah, it's a little funny."

"But you thought it was sad."

"It stayed with me. I stole a romantic moment between two people. It was a glimpse into everything I don't have."

"Oh."

"The worst was that I replayed it three more times. I could hear that she really did love him. The kids were great and thought he was the king, he could do no wrong. She'd planned ahead for him to come home and was counting the minutes. I got a small glimpse into something special."

Her head still on my shoulder, she wrapped her arm around mine and said, "You're such a romantic. Relationships aren't all that you think they are. There are good times and bad times, and you just try to do your best to get through them. You just got to hear a good time."

"When was the last time you called your husband like that?"

"We don't have that kind of relationship."

"No?"

"No. He's worried about me, we worry about one another, we share the same goals in life, and want to raise our kids a certain way. I wouldn't call him and swoon over new underwear I bought."

"You and I have a different relationship." I can barely get the courage to form the words. "If you and I had met in college...."

"Yes," she replies before I can finish. "Yes, if we had met before. But we didn't. We met when we did. Life is what it is. Mulligans are only in golf."

She turns her head up and looks at me with her deep green eyes. Slowly, I lean in and can only think "wonderful" as our lips press and she breathes the moment in deeply. I can taste the lip-gloss, wonderful; I can feel the smoothness of her skin, wonderful; our noses rub, wonderful, wonderful, wonderful. When I stop, she gives me half a smile and returns her head to my shoulder. I pull the small blanket from the back of the couch and lay it over her. We fall asleep watching the colored swirls slowly rotate, headed to our spot on the map.

A few hours later, at the peak of the storm, the winds wake me. She is still curled up and comfortable. I'm able to wiggle away from her, lift her up, and carry her to the bedroom located furthest from the storm's driving winds. When I finally get her under the covers she mumbles, "Don't go. Stay." Any romantic notions I might have, any opportunity I might take, could clearly happen tonight. But I go.

In the morning we meet again with the hotel management and come to an understanding. The storm hit south of us. The damage was minimal. Still, the airport won't open for another seventy-two hours.

I encourage Tatiana to rent a car and drive to Atlanta. She could be back home by night and planning for the next year the next morning. I'm not sure if she wants to stay, or is looking to me for an excuse, but I don't give her one. "What if" had kept me up all night after putting her to bed and "What if" had gotten me nowhere. She gives me a hug, offering once again to stay or take me with her.

Extending her hand, she shakes mine and asks, "How many is that now?"

"Number one," I say smiling. "You're always number one."

She smiles with a new glow. "One in a million?"

"You're much more than that," I say.

Lingering in that beautiful fragrance of hand lotion, perfume and whatever touch of magic she adds, I watch her go to the van that takes her away from me. I'm alone again.

Chapter 6

What your booth communicates is vitally important to the success of your marketing program. Many companies make the mistake of putting only their name and URL on the booth. Others believe in plastering the vibrant faces of happy models dressed as young professionals over everything. I'd always assumed this was to enable the onlooker to imagine him or herself in that delightful corporate world, but an image of a frazzled and exhausted man or woman is much more likely to represent the feelings of the trade show attendee.

In fact, it's rare that I see a beautiful professional. I have a big fat IT guy named Bob who wears his phone and pager like a utility belt and an HR lady named Rebecca whose odd frame forces her to lean to the left. These are real people with real challenges.

Here is what you should put on your booth: The name of your company, the logo of your company, and what you can do for the customer. The last is the most important and needs to be phrased in an engaging manner that addresses the top concerns the prospective customer has. Next, ask your question in big bold unforgettable letters: "Do you suffer from..." and fill in the blank. This could be easily adjusted to better fit the individual conference and the people in attendance. For

Comp-U-Soft the big question is "Do you suffer from bad data?" If you use any type of software, the likely answer is yes.

And by all means avoid the phrase "leading provider of" on your marketing message. I see this is on nearly every single booth and either it's just not true or it's inconsequential. Who are you fooling? There are eighty-seven companies on the floor and industry analysts rank you 86th. How are you a leader?

What we say to other people is just as important in life. I meant it when I told Tatiana that she was more rare than one in a million. But as a person who has literally shaken the hands of more than a million people, I should have met a second version of her by now.

On second thought, this would mean the order in which I met such unique people was sequential. In other words, that every one-millionth person is the unique one. She could just be one in a million, but I would need to go through 999,999 people to find the next one. Life can be so very random. I started the count with her. I don't think I will ever find someone like her again.

I'm in Vegas staying at the Hilton next to the convention center. There's a place in the hotel called *Star Trek: The Experience,* based on the television series and movies. There are games and a Star Trek-themed bar along with artifacts from the show and a "virtual experience."

Two years ago during COMDEX, the largest conference I attend, I made friends with a bartender at the *Star Trek Experience.* Dressed as an alien character called a Ferengi, with a large prosthetic forehead and enormous ears, he stands behind the bar on a riser. Once he is off the riser to grab a drink or walk the floor you realize he is five feet tall at best. I only know him as Phil the Ferengi, but he may be the best bartender I have ever met. He also owns a string of car washes.

"Hu-mon," he greets me in character, "what can I get you? Drink? Holodeck? Games?"

"Hello Phil, good to see you again."

"Ah, yes hu-mon, I thought I recognized you. What are you drinking tonight?"

"I'll have a gin and tonic please."

He steps up on his platform with the drink when he returns. I know I can talk to him because it's a slow night and I know his name.

"How are your travels, hu-mon?"

"They're good, thank you. How is your car wash?"

"They are very profitable. All of this desert dust can eat away at a car's finish. But there's also a new city ordinance; I have to "go green."

"What will that mean for you?"

"I have to add these tanks that collect used water, then filter it, and use it again. They call it gray water."

"I can imagine why."

"Are you sad, hu-mon? Or tired? You don't look well."

"I'm losing sleep. I've never had this problem before. I can usually sleep anywhere, but in the last week I can't get a full night."

"What's her name?"

"It's that obvious?"

"It is usually women or money. What's her name?"

"Tatiana. She is both unavailable and my obsession."

Phil grabs the bottle of gin and puts in on the bar in front of me. "Do you know Plato?"

"The philosopher? A little."

"Through Aristophanes, who was a peer of Plato's, we know this one interesting story about early hu-mons. Hu-mons were not separate from one another, but were made in pairs. They had two heads, four arms, and four legs. And they wouldn't walk around so much as they would roll around tucked up in a ball."

"This is not Star Trek?"

"No, ancient Greek philosophers describing the earliest version of humankind."

"Go on."

"So here they were—women and women, men and men, men and women—all sorts of these paired creatures rolling at great speed across the countryside of ancient Greece. The speed at which they move, the power they have, starts building confidence in humanity. The confidence turns to pride. And it's with this pride, what the Greeks call *hubris*, that they decide they are better than the gods and try to overthrow them."

A couple comes to the bar interrupting Phil and he takes their order. Once they are settled, he returns.

"So the hu-mons think they can conquer the gods. But when the hu-mons attack the gods, Zeus strikes them with such great power that he splits them all in two. Now the hu-mons are sad, desperate, and alone, and they start to kill themselves because they're having a hard time without the warmth and comfort of one another. Some remove themselves from the community. Others get lost in the wilderness and are never seen again."

"So what happens?"

"Zeus is wise. He and the other gods need the hu-mons to worship them. While they are asleep, he changes their bodies to what we know today, so that we walk upright and find it easy to reproduce."

"Interesting."

"Well, here's the part that applies to you, sleepy hu-mon. After all of those changes, the gods left a memory, a longing inside each of them for their other half. That craving for the other half is instilled so deep inside, that we end up traveling the world searching to fill that absence. And when we are fortunate enough to find that other half, we know instantly—getting lost in the entwinement of friendship and love and intimacy—that we have finally found home. People like this will spend their whole lives together. If you ask them what they find attractive or appealing about one another, they can't explain it—they just know it's right."

"It's a beautiful idea, that something is missing from each of us, and we have to trust others to fill that. I guess the heart wants what the heart wants; there's no getting around it."

"Easier to say, but I like my story better."
"Thanks for your time and the drinks," I say, getting up.
"Any time, hu-mon. We're always open."

Chapter 7

The drinks did not help. I may have gotten three hours sleep in total last night. I am irritable and cranky and I have to go talk to bankers for the next eight hours.

Normally I find banking shows enjoyable. There are all these silver-haired men of advancing years, escorted by beautiful younger women wearing large diamond-encrusted tennis bracelets. I'm not sure how they play tennis with so much jewelry on their wrists, but I've never been one to keep up with that sport.

Everyone loves Vegas, so today I have several volunteers from the office to work the booth. I have little to do but supervise and encourage the right things to happen.

A few minutes before the flood of bodies from the educational sessions fills the exhibit hall and the show floor gets busy again, a tall man with a lacrosse player's build comes up to me. From a quick look at his badge I see he's from our Canadian competitor SoftCom Data Services.

"Jim Stevens," he says, extending his hand to shake mine, number 1,002,616.

"Pleasure to meet you, Jim. I'm Peter."

"Oh, I know you very well, Peter."

"Really? I don't recall having met before. My apologies."

"We haven't met; I know you by reputation only. You're everywhere, man. You're at every trade show, every conference, and every exhibit in our industry. In fact, when I talk to people, your name comes up all the time. If someone isn't familiar with what we do, I ask if they've met you, and it comes back to them in an instant."

His Canadian accent is thicker than most. I suspect he grew up in Toronto, that he might even be second- or third- generation Canadian, an oddity in a city that is a mosaic of multiculturalism.

I smile and ask, "How can I help you, Jim?"

His polite exterior begins to melt as he tells me he wishes I would leave the industry. His voice grows louder as he says that my company is about to be acquired and that he'll be happy to see us torn apart in a corporate grinder.

Politely I ask, "Can we talk about this somewhere else—a private room, at the bar, outside?"

This only makes him louder and more hostile, and he begins to gather the attention of a large section of the exhibit floor. His rant now includes obscenities directed at me personally. In return I nod my head, calm, cool, the ambassador of software.

"Having a tough time competing with us, Jim?" I ask with an even bigger smile.

About to unload more venom, he suddenly becomes aware of the people staring at him as if he were a distraught homeless man fresh off the strip who'd walked into the exhibit hall with his shopping cart of crazy. He starts to flush with what I guess is embarrassment. He's silent now.

"Jim, have you got a business card? I'd be happy to follow up with you about this at another time and place."

He hands me his business card. I shake his hand again and put my hand on his shoulder, slowly walking him to the ballroom door where the event organizers have been watching with interest. Three large security men from the hotel arrive at the door behind the event staff.

"Jim, I'm sorry you're having a tough time. It's not an easy market with so many companies competing for business. I know you try hard. You have a lot of passion. But you should know this." The security men are now taking his arms. "If you pull that shit again at my booth, you will regret it."

Jim, while not breaking any laws, did not make the event organizers happy. Every time you sign an agreement to exhibit, you are tacitly consenting to follow a certain level of decorum.

Long after that incident, after the hours of standing and shaking hands, I'm in my hotel room. My laptop is on, my email answered, the paper work for the day complete. Jim Stevens's business card sits on the desk mocking me. I'm angry that a stranger would confront me at my booth, and I'm also worried—I don't know what's going on at the office and there might well be a merger or takeover on the way. If there was a sale or merger, I'm certain I'd be let go, without a home to go to.

I'm tired and Tatiana has been heavy on my mind. We've only exchanged email since Orlando, our weekly calls canceled at the last minute.

My anger, my exhaustion, my fear well up inside of me, and Jim Stevens is the outlet. So I start to type Jim's email address into a "free newsletter" registration. Jim will now learn more about the Church of Latter Day Saints. With a few more keystrokes, I sign Jim up for a dozen more daily and weekly newsletters about low home interest rates, pet supplies and grooming, and the national Communist party.

After three hours I feel much better. Jim is now part of 522 gay porn sites, 30 gender reassignment program alerts, 51 suicide prevention pep talks, and 48 requests for new car insurance quotes.

My phone rings. It's Tatiana.

"Hello?" I say, my heart beating fast.

"Oh, hey, I know it's late. I thought I might get your voice mail."

"Late for me? Late for you. What's up?"

"I got your email about Jim Stevens at the booth. There were also emails from the others at the booth, too. They said you handled the situation wonderfully, as I trust you always do. Did he really take a swing at you?"

"No, no, he was mad, raised his voice, yelled for a while and I walked him over to security."

"Oh, good. I was worried."

"That's nice of you, but I'm alright. If it were something more, I would have called and told you."

"Yeah," she says, searching for something else. "Well, I'm sorry I keep getting called into these last minute meetings. We haven't had a real conversation in a while."

"Since Orlando. I really enjoyed the time we had together."

"I did, too. It's rare that we get to see each other that much."

"Are you at home?"

"Yes."

"Everyone asleep?"

"Yes."

"How have you been sleeping?" I ask her.

"Bad. You?"

"Poorly when I get it. Which is unusual since I can generally sleep anywhere, any time I need to."

"It's dark and quiet here at the house. I couldn't sleep, so I wanted to call."

"I'm glad you did."

Before I could muster the courage to say something meaningful, something true, she wrapped up the call with a sniffle, saying, "Well, let's talk again soon. Take care out there."

It took me a second to figure out that she had been crying during that last part of the conversation. I couldn't call her back and wake the house. I wasn't brave enough to face these feelings and share them or put an end to them, for better or worse. There are so many things in life that we cannot say or express without thinking love will make us the fool. Instead, I can only linger in the renewed thoughts of "what if" and "what could be."

Chapter 8

People often ask me about the perfect handshake. Outside of practice, there's little I can teach you, but here are some pointers. It should last about three seconds. Keep your fingers together, thumb separate, and slide your hand into the other person's. It should be firm, not tight, and never a test of strength. Above all else, make good eye contact and smile.

What makes a bad handshake? Wet, clammy hands that are loosely grabbing at you or hands that tug only on your fingertips are the worst. Someone who cups or strokes your hand with the other hand, tries to grab your elbow, or does the manly half-hug is modeling behaviors better reserved for pick-up bars or for people with whom you are already intimate; they're just doing it wrong.

Other than that, the only advice I can give you is to keep a bottle of hand sanitizer with you or to wash your hands frequently. Travel means germs. Handshakes mean germs. Over time you'll build immunity to colds and flus, maybe even the plague, but it's much better to always be washing.

I'm in Phoenix, or PHX, which has my all-time favorite name for an airport—Sky Harbor. It sounds both futuristic and old-fashioned at once, calling to mind an age of flying cars or intergalactic travel while remaining grounded in something we've used for centuries with seafaring ships. It was the fourth airport in Phoenix and was built by Scenic Airlines, the outfit that flew over the Grand Canyon. It opened in 1929, right on the edge of the Great Depression.

Most of my time in the Phoenix area is spent at beautiful golf resorts in Camelback or Scottsdale just outside the city. Golf is a huge hook for event organizers. Every opportunity for pairs of executives in a shotgun start increases attendance and sponsorship. If I can put two of my guys on 18 holes of golf with two other CEO's or CFO's, it's easily worth $7,000 to $10,000 to me. The bigger the company I can spend that day with, the more I am willing to pay. It's all about building a relationship.

Unfortunately, this isn't one of those conferences. Instead I'm at a Marriott in the city. There are seventy-five people in a conference room for two days. When they eat breakfast or lunch, or take a coffee break, they join the event sponsors in a separate conference room next door. Most often there are at least ten of us packed in a room like this. Today there are three—Apollo Software, an older company that's a direct competitor, Comp-U-Soft, the company I work for, and Jim Stevens's company, SoftCom. This is an odd mix of old and new technology. I can't recall being stuck in a room with these other two alone before.

Solonge is my peer at Apollo. She has a few years on me; she's married and the mother of one, so she doesn't attend the same number of conferences and trade shows that I do. But who does? I only see her at the really big events. I'm not sure why she'd be at this one.

When I arrive, I find that, like me, Apollo has brought the standard tabletop display. This comes in one shipping box and can be set up in about five minutes. Very quick and easy. Very appropriate for this size audience. My display looks better and has a more relevant message, but hey, that's how I work.

SoftCom has gone another direction. They've sent a very large booth that fills a quarter of the room. It's lights are intense, the framework made of heavy wood, and the message a little off for this group. I'd estimate that sending this from Toronto and assembling it in this room cost them six thousand at a minimum. I doubt they'll make their money back in sales.

"Excuse me," I hear over my shoulder. "Are you Peter from Comp-U-Soft?"

I turn to find a young and friendly face. "I am. How do you do?" We shake hands.

"I'm Kim, from SoftCom. I think you met my boss Jim two weeks ago in Vegas."

"I did. How is Jim?"

"Jim's fine."

"Will he be joining us this week?"

"Well, I'm not sure. He was supposed to be here, but he's having all kinds of computer problems. Right after that event in Vegas our company email went down. Some strange cyber attack. It started with him and spread overnight to all the other sixty-two employees. Crashed the whole system."

"That sounds awful."

"It was. It was so bad that we had to re-build our email system and start to re-brand our contact information."

"Really? I've never heard of that before."

"Yeah, we had to start a whole new email address for everyone, re-print all of our literature with the new address, and update our website and business cards."

"Wow, that sounds intense."

"I haven't gotten my new cards yet, but here—" She hands me her business card. She's crossed out the old email address in pencil and written a new one above it.

"Thank you. I'm sorry, but mine are in my room. Stop by tomorrow and I'll be sure to give you one."

"Oh, that would be great." She pauses and looks at me with her head slightly cocked to one side. "You know, you're nothing like the way Jim describes you."

"Is that a good thing?"

"I don't know. I pictured someone much bigger and more threatening, but you're a big sweetie, all warm and friendly."

"I'm not sure what Jim told you, but I can assure you that I'm nothing more than what you see. I'm not out to get anyone or run my competitors into the ground. I'm just here to put my company in the best light."

"You know a lot about trade shows?"

"Yes."

"Maybe we could have a drink some time and you could fill me in on what I'm missing."

"That would be very nice. If not this trip, maybe the next."

"I'd like that. I'm in room 525. Call me if you want to grab that drink."

She is young, attractive, and I think she's flirting with me. When she walks away I can't help but notice her great legs, tight build, and slim frame. Why not have a drink? Not tonight, but maybe after the conference is over.

Chapter 9

My head hurts. I'm on the floor in a dark room. Slowly things become clearer. The bed's a mess. My room has been trashed. I have a sharp pain in my side and a dull one in my back and leg.

My head hurts more as I try to sit up. I decide to stay down and attempt to figure things out. I remember having drinks at the bar waiting for Kim, but she never arrived. There was another woman. I told her how alone I felt, how I hadn't been with a woman in at least five years. Was she a prostitute?

I hear water running in the bathroom. Someone's here. The hotel room door is ajar, held open by the locking bar.

She comes out of the bathroom, but all I can see is a shapely silhouette.

"Oh, you're awake."

"What happened?"

"Nothing fun, I'm afraid."

"Who are you?"

"You don't remember?"

"The girl from the bar?"

"Yes, Sarah Matthews. You and I were having a lovely time over drinks. You asked me to come back to your room, which I thought would be fun. But when we got to your door, this guy came from out of nowhere and hit you over the head."

"What?"

"He beat the shit out of you. Then he trashed the place looking for something."

"What?"

"Well, he left with your laptop."

"Did you try and stop him? Call hotel security?"

"Honey, just be still."

She sits down over me, placing a pillow behind my head and a cool washcloth on my forehead.

"Here, you had aspirin in the bathroom."

"Thank you."

"You said his name was Jim."

"Jim Stevens?"

"Yes."

"No. He's a competitor with anger issues."

I lie on the floor trying to make sense of things as this stranger sits over me watching.

Jim has taken all my plans for the next six months, all my history for the past year, if not more. Along with the thousands of photos of exhibit booths I've taken over the years, he has my only photos of Tatiana. She's standing in the background, moving her dark hair behind her ear, wearing a blue dress with white and black triangles in the pattern. Her ankle is slightly twisted and the light from the window's just right. It's the way I always like to think of her.

"Is it true? What you said about your boss? How crazy you are about her?"

"Did we talk about that?"

"By the fourth drink, that was all you were talking about. It's why I came up here with you. I don't know any guy who thinks about one woman that much."

"You'd think it was romantic, but she's married and unavailable. It's foolish."

"You said that, several times."

"There's no way this situation turns out well, no way I can see her being with me."

"You said that too."

"I'm a broken record?"

"You know, half of all marriages end in divorce."

"I know."

"But you don't want to be the reason for that."

"No. I must have said that, too. Why did you come up here?"

"I wished that someone felt as strongly about me. I know what loneliness is."

Hotel security knocks on the door. They enter the room and begin asking questions. I just lie on the floor listening to this woman explain the story again.

Another knock at the door, more security. Questions about calling a doctor or needing an ambulance. The name of the person who did this, a re-telling of the story, a phone call, talking into a microphone on the sleeve of the hotel staff, and the excitement of the situation all roll over me as I let others take control.

This is the payoff. My dedication and devotion to doing a job well has resulted in this isolation, loneliness, and abuse. I could care less about the laptop. I have a paper back-up at the home office I send each week for my files. I have a back-up disk with most of the things this week. And once I talk to Big Bob in IT, I'm sure I'll be back up and running quickly.

It's decided that they're going to help me up to the bed. Normally the advice is not to move the injured, but they feel I'm not complaining enough to be really hurt. They don't see any gushing blood. I do have some large bruises, a black eye, and a large lump on the head. I may feel worse from all the drinking.

By the time I'm on the bed and the staff has given me a good look, they decide not to call an ambulance. They've also gone to Jim Stevens's room, talked to him, and retrieved the laptop. He's now sitting in his room with the door blocked by security.

"So, would you like us to call the police? Would you like to press charges? We have the initial assault on video."

"Yes. Yes, please call the police. I think I'd like to press charges."

"Who was that woman?" Tatiana asked hours later.

"Which woman?"

"The one who called me from your cell phone and told me you were alright. Was she a police officer?"

"She was a witness."

"Oh."

"Nice lady. She was the one who confirmed Stevens attacked me. She called security, and apparently she called you, too."

"Are you alright? You sound distant, fuzzy."

"That's pretty much how I feel. I think I'm going to need a few days."

"She said you'd need to recover. How bad is it?"

"I don't know, I haven't looked in the mirror yet."

"Well, why don't you do that? I'll hold."

Slowly I make my way to the bathroom with the phone in hand. I look. It's worse than I thought.

"You know those maps of the world with the different countries colored deep purple, orange, yellow, and green?"

"Yeah."

"My face looks like one of those; it's a foreign landscape."

"Okay, that's it. I'm flying out there; I can be there at the end of the day."

"Tatiana, don't. It's just bruises. They're going to heal."

"But…."

"There is nothing you can do."

"But…."

"What about the girls? The house? Your husband?"

"But I…."

"I'm sorry that lady called you."

"Well, I'm glad she did. This is the kind of thing I need to know about. The kind of thing I want to know about. I want to know what happens to you. I care about what happens to you. More than just being your boss, or filling out the paperwork from HR, I care."

"Thank you."

"You're welcome."

"I care about you, too," I admitted with relief.

"I know."

"You do?"

"You're the one who doesn't seem to get it," she said. "Yes. Yes, I do care."

Chapter 10

Understanding your audience is vital to the successes of conveying your message. When I am talking with a senior level, or "C" level, person my conversations or presentations are about business strategy. How will this improve your overall business methodology for success? This is the question they want to know the answer to quickly. They will spend a great deal of money on consultants, pore through several of the top books, and attend conferences to see dynamic speakers to tell them how to improve. They're looking for one or both of two things-improved effectiveness and increased efficiency. How can I make the most happen with what I have at hand? How can I make incremental improvements to reduce errors and spend less to get an equal or greater return?

The mid-level managers, the next level down, belong to the group that actually puts these strategies into place. They are often handed a plan or directive and asked to carry it out and report back with weekly, monthly, quarterly, and annual statements of achievement. Directors and managers are often over-tasked with daily work, so these new plans and directives are not always well-received as they have likely gone through several of these in recent years. When speaking or presenting to this group, my message is not about strategy, but about operations and compliance. The oft-repeated phrase of President Clinton's, "I feel your pain," would apply to this group, which is also very appreciative of "tips and tricks" that will help.

I'm in Seattle, at the Sheraton on Pike and 5th, a great place for an extended stay. There's a very good barbershop and shoeshine on the premises. The beds are comfortable, the coffee is excellent, and the rooms are clean. I also appreciate the environmentally aware cleaning service here. My suits and shirts always return in great condition.

This event is targeting the third group in my audience, the people who actually install and support the software I sell. Due to the nature of constantly advancing technology, it's difficult to communicate with this level. It's nearly a foreign language at times, and they are quick to dismiss those who don't know as much as they do.

So I play to their other interests. Many people in this group like two things I'm also familiar with—comics and science fiction. So in order to answer a question or present ideas to this audience, I use references to these: "You know that part in Star Wars when they are in the Death Star and Obi-Wan Kenobi shuts down the main reactor?" "The '60s vision of future technology has finally arrived for today's businesses. This is the type of software Spock would leverage to understand the data on any planet, in any universe." "We are growing so fast in the amount of data we use, we have gone from bytes to kilobytes, megabytes, and gigabytes. Next we'll be into terabytes and petabytes – I would like to petition that anything after that we call Yodabytes."

When the taxi dropped me at the hotel I could tell the driver dropped my luggage hard. I'm not sure what I did to make him mad, or if he even knew what he'd done, though I've found most taxi drivers are very aware of the hard drop. If you don't tip well enough, they drop your roller bag on the wheels at a steep angle. This can crack the plastic wheels or bend the little axle that holds them in place. By the time I'd made it from the cab to the front desk for check-in I could already hear the click every few steps. When I got to the elevator my luggage wobbled like a bad shopping cart, and when I finally arrived at my hotel room on the 23rd floor the wheel had nearly fallen off.

Was Jim Stevens my first bit of bad luck? Was the hard drop and ruined luggage a second? I am reading too much into this. I have always been a fortunate traveler.

The Washington State Convention Center down the street is new and fresh and a wonderful place to hold a trade show. Built of glass and recycled building materials, it's interesting to the eye, there's enough room for everyone to be comfortable in smaller break-out rooms, and the exhibit hall is large but not overwhelming. The downside is location. Not many from the east coast or Midwest will think of going to Seattle over Vegas or Orlando. It's unfortunate really; they don't know what they're missing.

Booth set-up is quick and easy. I make certain my three tech-focused staff are checked in and ready to work. They're excited to see the keynote speaker, one of the tech world's top minds. There are also several sessions they want to attend. It's really a benefit to have them here, not only to work the booth, but to learn as well. This is one of the finer points I try to instill in senior management when pitching the idea of such a full trade show program. It helps with team building and creates a skill set that staff can bring back to the home office.

On day two of the three-day event, I'm alone at the booth between exhibit times. I've had my call with Kurt about pick-up, and next week, and something next month. Some of the booths are a little worn at the edges and we agree that after this season we might look to invest in properties that are lighter in weight to reduce the cost of shipping and drayage. We talk about the cost of repairing what we have, versus the cost of new properties amortized.

"Excuse me, are you Peter?"

I turn to find a man with graying hair in what I am guessing is his early forties. "Yes, I am." We shake hands, 1,003,003.

"I'm Frank Newhause, GlobalCom. Good to meet you."

"Nice to meet you, too."

"The event organizers told me you were here."

"I'm happy to help as best I can. What's on your mind?"

"Well, GlobalCom is a consulting firm of about fifty people, thirty-five of whom are actual consultants."

"That's a pretty good size firm. Why don't I know your name?"

"That's the thing. We've been around for eight years, we're growing, have several customers willing to give a positive reference, but no one knows who we are."

"That's a challenge. Where are you based?"

"Portland."

"North America? Or global?"

"Well, technically global, hence the name, but really North America."

"What can I do for you?"

"Are you happy at Comp-U-Soft?"

"Well, that's a loaded question. Yes, I'm happy there. I'm not in the office much, but I'm happy working for them."

"See, that's why I wanted to talk to you. I hear about your company all the time. And I hear about you; you're a legend in this industry."

"Well, that's really kind of you. I'm not sure what you've been told, or by whom, but I'm just a guy with a good product."

"You run the new business marketing program from hotel rooms."

"Yes."

"You're always on the road."

"That's true, it's the nature of the job."

"Your company has grown at an average of 14 percent year over year for the last five years."

"Well, yes, that's true too."

"This will be your sixth year with the company."

"I think you're connecting some dots here that aren't really connections. There's a team of people working with me."

"What are their names?"

"Sorry?"

"Who else is on the team?"

"I report to the director of marketing, a woman named Tatiana."

"And?"

"Well, like I said, I'm not in the office all that often; others process the leads I bring back, update the website, send out email, write literature."

"I see. I hope they're paying you well over there. It sounds like those people aren't bringing in new named accounts, but you are."

"Fred, what are you really asking me?"

"I need someone to make GlobalCom a recognized name in this space and I'm looking for the best guy out there to do it. Your name keeps coming up. I just wanted to meet you. Make sure you and I got to shake hands. Here's my business card. When you're ready to talk, you call me. Think about it."

"Thanks, Frank. I appreciate it."

Frank leaves me thinking. I haven't considered leaving Tatiana and Comp-U-Soft. Has it been five-going-on-six years? Or four-going-on-five? I know I'm pretty good at doing this, whatever this is called. So why don't I know the names of the other people on my team? Am I really a part of a team?

While my last time at a hotel bar hadn't turned out well, I venture down to the lobby of the Sheraton to work out some thoughts over a gin and tonic. Most times I just want to be silent in a room of people for a while. Talking with people socially after a long day of talking to people professionally can wear me down.

"Hey," says the man sitting next to me at the bar. "You here for this insurance convention?"

"No, just finishing up a technology trade show," I reply.

"I never thought I'd get into insurance; it seemed like a dull career path. But I was good with numbers and it paid well, and I got to be home for dinner every night of the week, so it fit in."

"You're a family man?"

"I used to be."

"Oh."

"Everything was going along pretty well. I was married for fifteen years, we had three kids, we had tough days, but nothing we couldn't handle together. I really loved my wife."

"That's great."

"I thought so too, until I got a phone call about four months ago. A phone call. She told me she'd met this guy three days earlier, that she'd fallen madly in love with him, and that she was going to leave me and the kids."

"Really? That's cold. A phone call?"

"Yeah."

"Now, wait. She'd met him only three days before and was now throwing away fifteen years of marriage and dedication to a family, for a guy she didn't really know."

"Yeah. That's pretty much it. We were divorced by the end of the month since she didn't want anything. It was the fastest divorce my lawyer and the judge had ever been a part of. Next day she married this guy and that was the end of it."

"What did you do?"

"I took leave. I took my teenage daughters to my parents' house and got on a flight. Went around the world over three months. I only got back last week."

"Well, going around the world sounds like fun."

"I was sad in London. I walked the Scottish countryside. When I got lonely I went to Amsterdam and spent a week crying in the arms of prostitutes I couldn't fuck. Eventually I made my way to Paris, where I finally felt I could make it through this situation. When I got to Moscow I was angry. It was cold, and different, and I didn't understand anything. From there I took the train south. I made my way to Turkey and traveled the Middle East. India made me appreciate everything I had. New Zealand was peaceful.

"That sounds like an amazing adventure."

Peter in Flight

"I stood at the edge of a cliff on the island of Hawaii, where the lava spills into the ocean, and thought about jumping in."

"Jumping in the ocean?"

"Jumping in the lava. It would have been a quick and painful death. A true sacrifice to the Polynesian gods."

"You were going to jump into a volcano? Over a woman?"

"Over my wife, my love, the mother of my daughters, the woman I trusted so totally I gave her my heart."

"What kept you from jumping?"

"My daughter called my cell phone."

"What did she say?"

"She told me to come home. So I did."

"Hawaii is nice."

"It is. When the girls are older, when they can take care of themselves, I might go back there."

"Lava sounds like as good a way to go as any."

"You understand?"

"Kind of. I often thought that I might run with the bulls in Spain, and when the time was right, just stop running and see what happened," I said.

"That sounds good, too."

"I think the trick is to make it look like an accident. Pulling the trigger of a shotgun with your big toe never seemed right to me."

"A frozen expedition to a mountain or the North Pole is much more appealing."

"And you don't want to just turn into traffic. You're going to destroy the lives of others; you just want it to be you."

"Yeah."

"But, still, you need to get home," I reminded him.

"Yeah."

"And eventually, the pain gets less and less powerful, like it happened to someone else, not you."

"Yeah."

"And those moments at Christmas with the girls, you want to see those happen again."

"Yeah, that's true."

"And you went through growing up with your parents. Would you want the girls to go through that? Would you want to put your parents through three more rounds of puberty and teenage life?"

"No, that's not fair to them."

"Wasn't there a woman?" I asked.

"What woman?"

"One in your office? The one who was pretty nice to you? Kind of interesting?"

"Oh, Samantha. Did I mention her?"

"She's what, divorced two years now, right?"

"Yeah, something like that."

"I bet she knows what you're going through. I bet if you called and asked her out, she might say yes."

"It's too soon."

"Hey, I'm not saying it's a commitment. It's the start of a conversation. Maybe she has a sister or friend. But you won't find out until you ask her out first."

"Yeah."

"Yeah, that's what I would do," I say. I nod and sip my gin and tonic.

"I might do that."

"I want you to do that tomorrow. Here's my card. You call me when that happens. I want to know how this story ends. If you book a flight to Hawaii, you call me. I'm going with you."

"Really?"

"Hell, yeah. I love Hawaii."

"Thanks, man. Thanks for listening—" He glances at the card, "—Peter. I really appreciate it."

"Any time. What was your name?"

"John, John Hall."

"John, give me your cell number. I'm going to add you to my cell phone. You call me when you ask Samantha out tomorrow."

"I will."

He gives me his number and I add him to my cell phone listing as "John Hall*DoNotLetGo2HI".

I understand John better than he might know. There have been many times since meeting Tatiana that I have weighed and measured the situation. Often I try to talk myself out of my feelings for her. The battle between head and heart is fraught with chemistry and forged through the fire of heated romance.

Love is made up of three chemicals—dopamine, norepinephrine, and oxytocin. From what I understand dopamine is the party drug. Its release makes you feel euphoric. Dopamine is the basis of sugary pop songs and overly romantic poetry. Dopamine is also the kick of cocaine. It's what puts you in the mood, but is entirely useless on its own, like mental masturbation. Dopamine needs norepinephrine. Norepinephrine communicates the good feeling you have between the little gaps in your brain, between neurons. This neurotransmitter is the part of love that brings focus and clarity to your world. When the rush of new love happens, norepinephrine makes the rest of the world melt away, allowing you to focus on the one and only thing. Norepinephrine is infatuation. Both of these chemicals are intense, like passions, which come on fast and leave quickly.

Finally there is oxytocin. After the rush, and the push and the pull, comes a long sustainable feeling. When the fire in your loins has faded, oxytocin provides a feeling of peace, stability, and companionship for a committed attachment.

This chemical cocktail is not equal parts. The cruel bartender of life has not stirred a balanced mix into everyone's drink. It sounds like John's former wife wasn't satisfied with her level of oxytocin. She found that rush of dopamine and norepinephrine in another man on first contact. That rush can be a powerful thing. I know. I feel it when I see

Tatiana. I drink in that intoxicating elixir of perfume and pheromones when she is near me. My heart beats faster when I hear her on the phone. In between those times I'm reminded of her husband, who could just as easily become someone like John. Lost and alone on the downside of a drug overdose that his own body made, he is trying to put back together some semblance of what he used to be before her. That high is so sweet on the way up, but cold and bitter when you come back down. I'm not sure who has it better—John, who will eventually find another person to help him replace that fix, or his former wife, who like a drunk that never stops so they won't feel the hangover, moves from one partner to the next, and will never feel that bad again.

Chapter 11

At about ten thousand feet you start to see the world dance across the ceiling of the aircraft; on a clear day it's even more detailed. Designers of modern aircraft have unintentionally built giant flying box cameras. Open windows become simple lenses that paint the interior surfaces as a moving canvas of an inverted world below.

The world today seems upside down to me. I'm grounded at the moment after a series of calls asking me to return to the home office.

Rebecca, the HR lady who cants slightly to the left, asked me to "return as soon as your last event ends." She said there was an "internal issue" we needed to discuss face to face. My first thought was of an acquisition, of losing my job. This was followed by a call from Jack Fowler, Tatiana's boss, the Vice President of Marketing. He also asked that I get back to the home office "right away," but went on to explain that "Tatiana was out indefinitely with a health issue," and I needed to run things for a while.

With the second call, my heart sank and a chill racked my body. I had never considered losing her. My mind jumped back to that late night call while I was in Las Vegas and she had been crying. Was there something she knew and couldn't say? We had talked since then, when she told me she cared. Had that been a good-bye?

The third call brought me back to earth after an hour of despair and anxiety and efforts to find the next flight home no matter the route.

"Pete?" It was Tatiana.

"Tatiana? Are you okay? What's happened?

"I'm fine." She sounded like she'd been crying.

"Tell me what's happened, please, I got a call that you were sick. What can I do? Who's the best doctor in this field?"

"Peter, I'm not sick. I'm fine. It's Yuri, my husband."

"Your husband's name is Yuri?"

"Yes. You didn't know that?"

"No, I just thought of him as your husband. What happened to Yuri?"

"He was driving south on the freeway along the lake after a day of golf. The police said there was a massive swarm of these may fly bugs on the road.

"Yuck, those things are smelly and greasy."

"Well, that's what happened. Those greasy bugs swarmed on the road, making a slick. He lost control of the car and went into this quarry. Paramedics were able to pull him out in time, but he's on life support in critical condition."

"Oh my god, Tatiana. I'm so sorry. You wouldn't believe what's been going through my head. I was so worried about you."

"I should have called you before Jack."

"That's okay. I'm just so happy you're alright." I was nearly in tears to hear her voice again. "What are they saying about Yuri?"

"They won't know anything until the morning."

"Where are the girls?"

"Here, with me."

"Where's his family?"

"They're on the way."

"When they get there, you should go home with the girls. Get some sleep. It's midnight here; it must be 3 a.m. there. You have to be exhausted."

"I don't know if I can."

"Okay. That's okay. Stay there with him. Do you have a friend who can watch the girls?"

"No, I mean, I would go home, but who knows what his mother would think. There's really nothing I can do here, so I'll have to play it by ear."

"I have the first flight out of Seattle and will be there in the afternoon."

"Alright." There was a long pause. "Can we just stay on the phone together?"

"Yes, of course we can. We can stay on the phone until our batteries give out."

"Thank you."

"Anything for you, Tatiana."

I could hear people in the hospital go about their nightly business in the background. Her breathing was regular, with the occasional shudder of emotion. Tatiana's mind must have been filled with questions and attempts at happy outcomes. This was one of those moments when I wished I could take her in my arms and tell her everything would be all right.

"Tell me a story," she said. "One of your tales from the road."

"I was in Atlanta last year, in Buckhead, at an event for four hundred people. The booth was set up, we'd been gathering names, showing off the product, and even had a customer speaker, a real bonus for that show."

"I think I know that event."

"There must have been sixty of our competitors there, all lined up to fight for the attention of attendees. One of the vendors was that small company based out of Portland, Comp-U-Stream."

"I don't think I know that one."

"Most of their team is nice, the product is buggy, and they only have eight customers right now."

"How do you remember this stuff?"

"I don't know. But your counterpart was there, the Marketing Director, this woman in her late forties, early fifties, built like a wood stove—short legs, long neck and a big block in the middle."

"Oh stop," she laughed. "That's cruel."

"During the conference, she was always trying to talk to me, trying to get my attention while I was working, which is annoying. When I finally paid attention to her, she started making these backhanded comments about our company."

"So what did you do?"

"Well, I was very nice to her, gave her no reason to say bad things or believe we were bad people."

"Well, that's not much of a story."

"Well, you have to wait."

"So go on."

"So, I'm dismantling the exhibit and she's standing there flapping her jaw, watching me take the booth apart, put it into the case, fill out all the forms, and lug it over to the shipping desk."

"And what's she doing?"

"Following me like an imprinted baby duck. Then, when I say good night, because it's eleven o'clock at this point, she says she doesn't know how to take apart her booth."

"What?"

"She's been bugging me the whole time, waiting, just to ask me to help her take apart her booth and ship it for her."

"Doesn't she know she can hire someone to do that?"

"She's an idiot. She has no idea what's going on. But I'm a nice guy, and she's in no shape to do this on her own. We walk over to her booth."

"What kind is it?"

"It's one of those really easy pop-up frames. We have one just like it, and it's a twenty-minute job. As I start to disassemble the thing, I notice that she's walked away. I'm not "helping" her; I'm taking the booth down on my own. You know those little plastic bits that are easy to break and expensive to replace?"

"Yes."

"I broke them."

"No."

"Yes, I popped those little buggers and broke each one of them."

"Well, you can't put the booth up without those."

"I know. Then, all the graphic materials that you need to roll up in a certain way—the ones that clearly state 'Do Not Roll Graphic Face In'—I rolled them graphic face in."

"Stop."

"For the kicker, when I filled out the paperwork for shipping, I sent it to Anchorage, Alaska for a very expensive trip."

"You are so bad."

"If they're even able to find the booth, they'll need to spend about $8,000 just to fix it, and another $1,500 to ship it back."

"You're a monster," she teased. "I don't want to ever be on your bad side." She laughed.

It was good to hear her laugh. I was happy to take her mind off the moment. We talked a little more about the girls and gymnastics. The older one was winning ribbons and trying to teach the other girls during recess how to do cartwheels.

Soon, from her long pauses, I could sense she was drifting into sleep. I imagined that she had curled up on a couch or chair with the phone resting near her ear. With just those few moments of relief from thinking about Yuri, and the kids, and what was going to happen with the rest of her life, her mind had slowed down enough to sleep. I stayed on the phone and listened to her breathe. Once in a while I could hear her lick her lips or start to snore a little. As she started to dream, I turned on my laptop to find those few cherished photos I carried with me. There she was in that blue dress, moving her dark hair behind her ear, with the light just right, her foot poised slightly at an angle from those years of ballet, and thin lips outlining her wonderful smile. I could not imagine losing her.

Chapter 12

I think of Detroit as my home, though I've never really lived there. I was born there, and grew up outside the city, but Detroit still seems like the place my life began, since it's where the office is. Most people in southeastern Michigan live in the suburbs, like I did, not in Detroit. Though some of my hip high school peers have become "urban resettlers", moving to the city in an attempt to rebuild it, they are a small and brave few.

When I get to the office, it's late afternoon. I meet with Jack and go over his priority list. I meet with the office manager and get the key to Tatiana's office. When I sit at her desk, I breathe in deeply the lingering fragrance of when she was last here. It warms my heart.

From her desk I can see right into the cubical I used to sit in, an interesting revelation on perspective. I wonder what her thoughts about me might have been those first few months.

The password and login that she gave me work fine, and her computer whirs up to speed to announce with a little tune that it is up and running. On her desk are photos of the two girls, who smile at me from two years ago when the photo was taken. But there's no photo of Yuri. The top drawer holds supplies, the middle drawer files, and the bottom drawer is provisioned with peanut M&M's, granola bars, bottles of water, tampons, tissues, an extra pair of socks, and a photo of the two of us from four years ago. I'd forgotten it had been taken, but still, there we are, standing next to one another wearing cowboy hats in front of a mechanical bull just outside of Dallas, Texas. It's another interesting revelation on perspective.

Once inside the computer, I spend the next three hours going through email based on project folders and forward them to myself. I turn on her "out of office" notification, alerting anyone attempting to contact her that they should instead contact me. Once I have things in place and am confident that I can move forward with Jack's game plan, it's tempting to look around the rest of her computer.

Perhaps this is over the line. Maybe it's one of those minor sins like looking inside another person's medicine cabinet. Nevertheless, I take the opportunity and quickly scan through the photos on her hard drive. The only non-work-related pictures are of her daughters, and the one of us in her desk drawer.

She keeps a separate email folder for everyone she works with, every message sent or received between the two. She never throws out a thing. My folder is full of email I've already gone through but from the opposite perspective. Yuri's folder is where I'm crossing the line, so I only look at subject headings like "Late for Dinner," "Your Turn to Pick up Girls," and the riveting "Late for Dinner Again." In the drafts folder, I find unfinished thoughts that have not yet been sent. There are several here pertinent to the projects I'll be picking up, just in need of final details. I forward them to myself.

One email is addressed to me, and was started shortly after the hurricane in Orlando. I know I should not read it, but I do.

"Peter – I should have stayed in Orlando. There was no rush to get back here and not much to get back to. Things at home have been different for a while now and you seem to be the only person who understands me or sees me as more than a chauffeur, a cook, or the bad guy when it comes time for decisions. I wish there were mulligans. I wish we had met in college."

Yuri looks different than I imagined he would when I deliver flowers later that night. Who knows how he wore his hair before, but now his head has been shaved, with a large fresh scar running across the right lobe and staples holding it tight. His eyes seem swollen shut rather than peacefully closed. He has a breathing tube in his mouth, a heart rate monitor on his finger, and all sorts of wires running to a spot on his chest. There must also be a catheter running to the empty collection bag on the side.

Either I've just missed the nurse or his systems are starting to shut down. A saline solution or some other concoction runs into the port on his chest. He's also sporting inflatable socks to promote circulation in the legs and prevent deep vein thrombosis.

He looks much like my mother did for those last six months they kept her alive. Once they found the brain tumor and removed it, it was all downhill. A slow and steady beep that eventually faded. I was too young to make any decisions, Dad had died years earlier from lung cancer, she had no other family, and so she ended up a ward of the state. The hospital followed policy from that point on and kept me informed during my daily visits. There comes a time when they just can't do anything more and there are no promising signs of life. I learned your choice is to have a living will and end things fast, give it some time to see if a recovery to a certain quality of life can be achieved, or let people hold on to hope for decades while the body functions.

We've gotten so good at medicine that we're able to keep the machine of the body running to imitate life well past a true expiration date. How to act at the end of life might be the cruelest lesson humanity has yet to learn.

"Hello," a female voice says behind me. "Are you a friend of Yuri's?"

I turn to find an attractive young blonde with a tiny frame, stiches on her forehead, and a black eye.

"Ah, yeah, I'm Peter. And you are?"

"Tammy Lynn."

"Nice to meet you, Tammy Lynn. I was just dropping off some flowers from the office, but they said not to go in the glass room—it's sterile. I guess I'll leave them here."

"That's very nice of you guys. I don't think we've met before. I'm kind of new. Are you in the front office with Yuri?"

"Tammy Lynn." I stall for a moment, realizing she thinks I work with Yuri. "Why does that name sound familiar?"

"I'm new in the accounting department. I do the books with Ruth."

"Ruth, accounting, yeah." I shake my head up and down. "Are you okay? You've got some stitches and bruises too."

"Well, thank goodness I didn't get the full force of the hit. My airbag went off. Poor Yuri, his didn't."

"Poor Yuri." I shake my head in sympathy.

"When the paramedics arrived, they were able to resuscitate him, but maybe I should have left him in the car to sink to the bottom of that quarry. He would have been better off."

"Yeah, well, you did your best. Did you meet his parents earlier?"

"No. Well, no. I tried to come later to avoid the family. I didn't want to meet them like this...."

"Yeah."

"...with the divorce and all."

"Divorce?"

"Yeah, I guess his wife is a real witch, and they separated last year, and have been going through some nasty divorce."

"I didn't know that. Poor guy," I say. *Poor naïve girl,* I think. Or am I the naïve one?

"Well, I'm going to leave this here. It was nice to meet you, Tammy Lynn."

"Nice to meet you too, Peter."

Peter in Flight

Walking past the registration desk, I hear my name called. It's Tatiana. We hurry to each other and I hold her in my arms tightly.

"It's so good to see you," she says.

"I'm so happy to see you, too."

"What are you doing here? You should have called."

"Well, I got some flowers and dropped them off, looked in on him. I didn't want to bother you. I know you're busy with everything."

"Thank you for coming."

"You're welcome. Where are the girls?"

"With his mother. They keep her busy; she's pretty sad to see her son like this."

"And his dad?"

"Has hardly said a word for days. Just stands around, waiting for news."

"Can I get you some really bad coffee?"

She laughs and smiles, looking warmly into my eyes. "No, no, thank you."

"Water?"

"No, thanks, I'm good. It's so good to have you here. Do you want to go up with me for a while?"

"Oh, you know, let's give it a moment. I think the nurse was changing something or switching something when I was up there."

"Yeah, they just walk in all the time."

"You have to be certain they wash their hands," I warn.

"Why?"

"There are germs and disease they carry with them all the time, from room to room, and spread to other patients. Some of them are not as good as others at washing their hands. You have to be certain they wash."

"Okay. You've spent some time around hospitals?"

"I have. People get sick staying here, not just before coming here."

"Okay. I'll keep an eye on that. Let's run up there real quick and tell the nurse to wash her hands." She takes my arm and starts to drag me toward the elevators.

From a few yards away I can see it coming. The elevator pings, the doors open, and out steps Tammy Lynn.

"Hi, Peter," Tammy Lynn says walking past us.

"Hi."

Once the elevator door closes, the question from Tatiana follows.

"Who was that?"

"Tammy Lynn. I met her a few minutes ago on Yuri's floor."

"Oh."

And that's the end of it. A short and simple "oh" and we're in front of Yuri's viewing wall where I had left the flowers.

"These are nice. Thank you."

"You're welcome."

"He looks the same as when I left. The nurses and doctors are still just saying 'wait and see' with his condition."

"Did they operate on him?"

"No, they just mended his head from the crash."

"Is he bald?"

"Yeah, that's funny. You've never met. You don't know what he normally looks like."

"Well, I'm sure he's a handsome man when he's standing up."

"He has his good points."

We stand silently for a while watching the respirator fill his lungs and then let the air escape. The head nurse eventually comes by to tell Tatiana what I suspect they've been telling her all the time, steady but critical condition, wait and see if he comes out of it.

I tried to keep Tammy Lynn out of my mind. For all I knew, maybe they had separated and were in the process of filing for divorce. Some couples are funny that way—they don't tell anyone until the deed is accomplished.

Peter in Flight

Yuri was sleeping with the new girl at work, they were out for a fun time when the crash happened, and no one told Tatiana that there was someone else in the car. Why would they?

An hour later I find myself in front of Tatiana's car giving her the best hug I have ever given anyone. She must be able to feel each beat of my heart. I hold her tight and whisper positive things in her ear—like "It's going to be all right" and "We're going to figure things out." I don't really care if they are true or not. I believe them and hope she will too.

It's late when I watch her drive away and I get into my rental car to drive back to the hotel across the parking lot from the office. Waking up and going to the office will be an interesting experience for me. It's been a while since I reported for duty.

Chapter 13

"Who was that?" she asks, standing in her office door.

"That was a friend of mine, John Hall. He was calling to let me know he was getting married, and that I should save the date."

It's strange to see her in the office again, strange to be sitting at her desk and watching her stand at the door. There's something so alluring about her leaning in the doorframe with her hair in a ponytail and wearing that navy sleeveless dress with the red belt. She loves those red heels and wears them at every opportunity.

"Don't get too comfortable in that chair."

"I'm just keeping it warm for you."

"I stopped by to update Jack on things."

"And?"

"Since last night, unchanged. Since the accident, unchanged."

"So you're saying nothing's changed?"

"No, smart ass," she says with a smile.

"What will you tell Jack?"

"As things aren't changing, I might think about coming back." She steps inside and closes the door behind her. "That would be great."

"You think so?"

"If you're ready for it, yeah."

"I don't want to be a bad wife, or poor example of a mother, but I can feel the edge of my talents slipping away. And I don't like that feeling."

"Wanting to be back at work doesn't make you a bad wife or mother."

"I think people expect me to be there twenty-four hours a day, just in case he comes out of it, like I need to be the one he wakes up to."

"But you don't?" I ask.

"I don't. I don't feel that need. The hospital will call me if that happens."

"If?"

"I'm not giving up hope, but let's be realistic about this. The prognosis isn't good."

"If the situation were different and you felt you were talking him through it, that he knew you were there…." I say.

"Exactly. If he were semi-conscious, or there was more than the parade of doctors and nurses coming through his room at all hours, it would be different."

"Do you think you need a break yourself? A holiday, a vacation from things?"

"I just want to get back to some level of normal."

"You know, when you come back, people here are going to be walking on eggshells. They're going to treat you differently," I say.

"Yeah, I guess, but it will be closer to normal."

My smile is a bit forced. "Then I say do it. Get back here before you lose that edge."

"Really?"

"Hell, yeah. Go tell Jack; get back in here."

Her smile is real. It's precisely what she needs, too, a sense of stability, a distraction from practically living in the hospital. My constant buzzing around her, our late-hour phone calls and coffee-filled conversations over the last few weeks have been great for me, but now it's time to fly. That corporate apartment I've been stuck in, with that stupid rental car and regular schedule have been slowing me down. Now who was being naïve?

Chapter 14

It's a beautiful Tuesday morning in September for my triumphant return to Trade Show World. Traffic to DTW is light and I make good time dropping off the rental car. I feel a huge relief to move out of the corporate apartment and back into my routine of handshakes and product demonstrations.

This respite of spending every day with Tatiana, while wonderful, has been only fleeting. Her husband will eventually wake up, her life will go back to normal, and I will remain alone in first class with regular upgrades to my hotel rooms. If loneliness creeps back into my life, I won't be like John Hall and seek out a glorious end, but accept the invitation from another traveler to find comfort in each other's arms for the night, or call a service to relieve that built-up tension that plagues my kind. I'll live up to the image of having a girl in every port, like the previous generations of tradesmen who came before me.

In the terminal of DTW, my habits fall back into place quickly. I'm through the metal detector and off to the executive lounge for a quick coffee; my flight is called minutes later and I'm on board the Boeing 767, ready for taxi. The plane's not full yet the cabin door is closed, and we start to roll quickly down the runway. I'm ready to leave the last six weeks behind and return to the road. It will be a long flight to LAX.

Just as the roar of the engine picks up, acceleration pushes me back into my seat, and the nose begins to lift, the pilots pull an emergency cut to the power. The nose drops hard back to the runway and there's a violent shift to the right as the entire plane rapidly moves from the runway back to taxi. The plane comes to a halt in an unfamiliar area.

Silence fills the cabin. Passengers begin to look to one another for answers no one has. Slowly the sounds of beeps and whirs from cell phones being turned on take place. I am one of the first with mine. Within seconds of activation, there's call from Tatiana.

"Hello?"

"Are you alright?"

"Yes, our plane didn't take off. Why? What happened?"

"There was a plane crash in New York. A plane hit the World Trade Center. I knew you were flying today and wanted to make certain that you were okay."

"I'm okay."

"It looks like King Kong punched a hole in one of the Towers."

"I never understood why New York and Tokyo were always the targets of monster attacks, at uncommonly high levels," I say to lighten the moment. "When will other major cities get their turn?"

Her laugh quickly turns to a chilling, "Oh my God."

"What? What is it?"

"Another plane, the other tower."

All of the cell phones on the plane are now ringing or engaged in conversation.

"Another plane? I don't understand."

"We're under attack." She went silent while attempting to understand the gravity of the moment. "You should come back. I don't think you're going anywhere. Call me when you get settled."

I don't fully realize the magnitude of my comment's inappropriateness until I see the images on the executive lounge television. Everything at the airport is closed except this one spot where I stand and watch the confused reports from across the east coast before returning to the car rental. I find that my exalted status doesn't matter; there are literally no cars left on the lots at any of the agencies. The smart travelers are already on the move, driving away from here and trying to get home. I've become slow and rusty from my weeks in domestication.

As I weigh my options—find a taxi and go back to the corporate apartment; stay at a hotel near the airport; hitchhike to wherever I can get to—a young man from my preferred car rental desk catches up with me.

"Peter?" he says, nearly out of breath.

"Yes."

"I found a car for you. They're driving it over from another lot. If you can follow me back to my desk, we can take care of the paperwork."

"Thank you."

"You're welcome."

"No, really. Thank you. What's your name?" I extend my hand.

"Jimmy Newbrook." Number 1,003,911.

"Jimmy, you don't know how big a help this is."

"Well sir, to be honest, with your status, something in the computer clicked over and told me to find you."

"I appreciate the honesty. But you still tracked me down."

It's a huge black Lincoln with everything. In the car, driving back to the apartment, I tune into Howard Stern and listen to the cries and plight of New Yorkers as they call in. I can hear the honest and genuine concern and uncertainty in Stern's voice. The news seems more real when I hear it from him, and I think how odd it is that things work that way.

I'm in tears when I pull into the parking space; for an instant it seems my world is falling apart. Who knows when I'll be able to fly again? If what they are saying is true-that we are under attack-there'll be a war and it will be a long time before the next trade show or conference. The woman I love is still unobtainable, maybe more so now than ever, as she waits for her husband to wake up from a coma.

Chapter 15

"I miss being a child," she says in my arms as we lie on the couch of my corporate apartment in front of the television. "No worries. People there to look after me. Thinking that I knew everything, but not knowing much about life."

"I know what you mean," I say.

The moment reminds me of our last trip to Orlando. The news has been repeating itself for several hours, inching forward to the morning when we hope there would be something new. We've each had a couple of drinks that have loosened the state of our minds. Outside there's the chance of impending doom. The only comfort I have is the weight of her body on me and the soft sweet smell that wraps around her.

This time there's no phone call from her husband to interrupt, no voice in my head making the case to stop. Only the questions: If not her, then who? If not now, then when?

Her head lifts from my chest and she looks at me with those beautiful eyes. I lean in and give her a long hard kiss while taking her in my arms. Her soft and wonderful lips are warm and inviting. Soon our mouths open and the deep breathing of early passion begins to rise. I caress her breasts and my hands find new places to touch.

Peter in Flight

"Let's take our time tonight," she says. "It's been a few months since I've done this."

"Yeah, sure, it's been a few years for me too," I reply.

She stops. She sits up with a surprised look on her face.

"A few years? Like how many years?"

"I don't know, a few. Why are we stopping?"

"Well, how long has it been?"

I pause to think about the last time I actually was with a woman. It was something of a weekend thing when I was at the shore, visiting friends in New Jersey.

"You have to think about it? It must have been a while," she continues.

"I've not been with anyone since before you and I first met. Whatever it is that you and I have may have been something that you've come to realize during our time together, but for me, I knew when we first met—in an instant—that I was crazy about you."

"That was almost six years ago. You've been celibate for six years? Waiting for me?"

"Well, yes. I never thought of it that way, but yes."

"It's only been maybe six months for me."

"That's okay, isn't it?"

"All those years I was with Yuri, and you were waiting?"

"I tried not to think about it in those terms. I tried not to imagine you in the arms of another man." Unfortunately, this reminds me of a business card I keep in my desk.

"Why didn't you say something? Why didn't you tell me how you felt?"

"You were married—you are married—you're a mom, and you're my boss. You have this whole other world to consider, and I—well—I have me. I could wait. You're worth waiting for."

She has a puzzled look on her face as she takes the small blanket from the back of the couch and retreats to the corner of the sectional, as far away from me as she can get.

"And now you can't wait any more?"

"I can wait. I thought this was something you wanted, too."

"I do."

"But?"

"I need to process this, understand first, before I can."

"Ask me anything."

"Have you ever lied to me?"

"Yes."

"About what?"

"I knew the hurricane was coming but said I didn't. Every time there was a chance to tell you how I felt, I went in the other direction in the conversation."

"More recently?"

"I told you to come back and work in the office, knowing I'd have to leave you again, but I didn't want to leave you. This has been the most time I've gotten to spend with you. And I've loved every minute of it. I hope that doesn't make me a bad person."

The smile my words elicited returned to suspicion quickly. "Nothing else?"

"I know better than to bring it up—I know that it will end the evening—but believe me, I'm interested in the success of our long-term relationship, not just-well- sleeping with you."

"This sounds bad. Is it bad?"

"Yuri wasn't alone in the car when it crashed."

"What?"

"When you and I were at the hospital that first night I was in town, we met a young woman named Tammy Lynn. She was a passenger in the car with Yuri. She pulled him out of the car. Her airbag deployed but his didn't."

"I don't understand."

"Tammy Lynn said that you and Yuri had been separated for the last year, that the divorce was about to come through. Is that true?"

"No."

"I don't have evidence, but I believe that Yuri was cheating on you."

"What? No! We had our problems, but…."

With that, the bright pink bra I've spent the last six years trying to get a better look at disappears under her blouse. Her perfume lingers a good five minutes after she slams the door, leaving me alone again.

Chapter 16

Throngs of people can be overwhelming. The pressing of bodies against each other generates a certain heat, a unique aroma. After hours of standing on a poured cement floor with nothing but a half-inch-thick piece of carpet as padding—the more fortunate rest on an inch of foam—you can feel the burn in your calves. Your feet swell. Your eyes and throat become dry. Still, the masses want to meet you, shake your hand, and grab your free giveaways. This is what you can expect at the big shows.

The absence of these masses is even worse. All that you can think about are your bloated feet, sore back, and a perfectly stacked pile of giveaways that are taunting you.

I'm in Chicago at McCormick Place, one of three convention centers that trade the title of being the largest in the U.S. each year. Of the series of interconnected buildings that house some of the biggest trade shows, we're in the once closest to Lake Michigan, with all the large windows overlooking the small airport.

Over the last five years, this event has had a steady increase in attendees; this year we're expecting fifteen thousand. So far I've talked with three people. One of them is the very attractive girl from Texas representing Enron at the booth across the aisle from me. Her name is Cathy McKinley, 1,004,412. She started with Enron three weeks ago, fresh out of college; she's a Longhorn, and is super-excited about this opportunity.

The other two people I've met are down the aisle from my booth. One is giving away a "Big Bertha" golf driver, and the other is giving out sleeves of golf balls with his company logo on them. They're currently taking turns making full swings with the club to pass the time. While no windows have been broken yet, a large group of exhibitors with nothing to do has gathered just to stand and watch, waiting for the next thing to happen.

It's my first trip since September 11th—well, since July actually. Tatiana and I mostly communicate through email these days. It's nearly all about business. I don't know if she's mad at me for not telling her right away, or just mad at Yuri. Probably both the men in her life have let her down more than she deserved. There's no easy way out of this situation. That much is certain.

Normally I wouldn't take a call at the trade show booth; it's one of the unbreakable commandments—along with no eating, drinking, or smoking. However, with the slow pace of things I make an exception.

"Hello?"

"Peter?"

"Yes."

"This is agent Frank Thornton with the FBI. May I have a moment of your time?"

I get a chill from hearing those three letters, FBI. I must have done something wrong, or someone is in danger.

"Certainly. How can I help you, agent Thornton?"

"I got your number from the airline, you were originally booked on American Airlines Flight 11 from Boston's Logan Airport to Los Angeles International Airport on September 11, 2001. Is that correct?"

"I'm not sure; I'd have to check my records."

"We show that you booked a seat on that flight on May 15, 2001, but cancelled that flight in July. The reason for my call is to find out why you cancelled that reservation."

"Oh. I travel extensively for my job as a marketing manager of trade shows. Originally I was scheduled to go from a conference in Boston to another event in LA. However my supervisor's husband was in a car accident, and I was called back to the home office in Detroit to fill in for her while she was out tending to him."

"I see."

"Listen, you can call her. Her name is Tatiana, and I'll give you her direct line. I'll also give you the number of her supervisor, Jack Fowler, who actually called me and asked me to come back to the office."

"That would be good."

"If you give me an email address I can forward confirmation that I was asked by my employer to change flights, if that's alright."

"That would be acceptable."

"Why is the FBI calling me?"

"Oh, hi, Tatiana. Good to speak with you, too."

"What kind of trouble are you in? Why are they asking about Yuri's accident?"

"They wanted to confirm that I was originally booked on American Airlines Flight 11 to LAX the one that hit the World Trade Center's north tower—and that I cancelled the reservation because I was coming back to the office after the accident."

"Oh."

"I'm sorry to put you through this, but I gave them your name and Jack's to confirm what happened."

"You were scheduled on that flight?"

"I've been scheduled on all kinds of flights, Tatiana."

"No, that's a big thing, Peter. You were going to be on that flight out of Boston."

"Yeah, I was." An awkward amount of silence and I change gears in the conversation. "Maybe we do get mulligans in life. Maybe there are do-overs."

"Maybe."

We stay on the line for a bit without saying anything. I want to tell her how sorry I am, how awful I felt being the messenger. I want to tell her how important I thought it was that she knew, not to divide her and Yuri, but just to know she wasn't a bad person for wanting to be back at work. I want her to know that I didn't tell her at the time because she already had too much going on, and that her life was already complicated enough.

She breaks the silence. "So how's the show going?"

"It's empty. Fifteen thousand people didn't show up. All morning there were two guys driving golf balls two hundred yards down the aisle until the event organizers came and had them escorted out of the building. Then, about an hour ago, the new booth person at Enron named Cathy got a call from her boss and walked away from the booth."

"She did what?"

"She got a call from her boss saying that Enron has just gone under, that Cathy had just lost her job, and that her corporate credit card might not be working any more. So she just walked away from the booth. She was going to try and get on the next flight home."

"Wow. These are strange days."

"Strange days indeed."

"What's next?"

"Well, Tatiana, the easy answer is that you forgive me, and we go back to being best friends. It's awful without you in my life."

"I meant which show are you going to next?"

"Oh. I'm going to be in Manhattan tomorrow."

"Okay."

"It's a small conference, a hundred people, all local. I called the event organizer and he told me he'd called the entire registration list and got 90% of them to confirm they were still coming."

"After that?" She had her disappointed mom voice on.

"I'll be back in the office after that."

"Maybe you should think about getting an apartment of your own when you get back. I'm not sure my marketing budget can do another run of that corporate living thing without revenue coming in."

"I understand."

"Okay."

"Hey, I'm really sorry."

"I know. It's just not that simple."

"I know."

"Get back here safely. We can talk then."

The pilot takes a new route into LGA on his approach. My window overlooks the column of smoke down into the rubble as he banks at the tip of Manhattan to make the turn. Nearly everyone on the other side of the plane has undone their seatbelts and leaned over to get a better look.

Television has done a good job in showing the images of a thick layer of dust that covers everything. There's a deep pit with wreckage poking out in every direction and a high level of activity on the ground.

What television could never convey was the smell that permeates the city. From my first step out of the taxi, it fills me with a distinctive sense of dread. It has a bitter sting—the odor of a campfire with electrical wires thrown on top of it.

This is the first time I've attended this conference. Its organizer is a pear-shaped man in his fifties who has tried to shave his few remaining hairs, only to miss one or two very long strands. It's the only thing to look at when attempting to avoid staring at the mounting piles of dandruff on his shoulders.

The event is as he'd described: one hundred attendees from the New York area who are a perfect match for our products. I spend the day meeting seventy-two of them, discussing their needs, shaking hands, and exchanging business cards.

Peter in Flight

By the end of the day, having time to think things through, it becomes apparent that things have changed and might never return to what they used to be. Me, Tatiana, trade shows, travel, my world, the world, it might never be the same.

Chapter 17

Jack Fowler's office is what you would expect from any sales executive. The leather couch is thick and lush. His walls are frosted glass up to a certain height for privacy, but, when he's standing, he can look out and survey the efforts of his minions. The window to the outside world has a view others envy, yet it's a view he rarely sees.

He pours me a stiff drink from the bar hidden inside a globe he purchased from Sky Mall two years before. "Peter, did I ever tell you how I got started in this business?" he asks.

"No." I lie. I've been told this story dozens of times. I've been present even more often in the telling of this tale to others. The dates change. The moral to the story fits the moment. I know this story.

"I started my career in software—what is it now? twenty-five-years?—loading tapes on the midnight shift in the data center. After six months of proving myself, I moved on to an opportunity in sales. Sales can make you a man, Peter. A good sales person needs to know two things. You know what they are?"

"No." I lie again.

"Product and people, Peter. It's all about product and people. I've always liked that about you. You know our product as well as any programmer, but you can't program. And you sure know people. You know people inside and out. But your politeness prevents you from being aggressive enough for sales."

"Well, I certainly appreciate that insight. It's always good to get perspective on how one can improve." Again, I lie.

"Peter, you've done good work for us over the years and I appreciate that. But with recent changes in our world, it doesn't look like we're going to be doing the types and nowhere near the number of events that you are so skilled at. I'm giving you the gift of finding a new opportunity with a new employer." He says this with a quick coldness that comes from rehearsal.

"You see, our company is being purchased. The new owners are going to announce it at 4:00 p.m. this afternoon. This company is going to come in and make things more efficient around here, streamline things."

I stop him before he can finish what he practiced in the mirror all morning. "They're buying this company for the 14 percent year-over-year revenue increases, the ones you could not have gotten without the huge number of new named accounts I brought in from living on the road."

Jack has perfect hair. When I first met him it was black and thick, shaped with care. Now it has a saltiness to it that makes him more sophisticated and mature.

In spite of this hair, this handsome man of six-foot- something shakes his troubled head with regret. "I know that, Peter, and I think you did a hell of a job." He over-articulates it again. "A *hell* of a job. If I had more trade shows and conferences to send you to, I'd send you out there and let you do your magic, shovel those leads into us, stoke the fires of the engine. But it's not there. It's just not there."

"Well, Jack, I guess you have to do this. It's the best business choice we have."

"If you were this talented at something else, if I could use you in another spot, another department, I'd keep you on. I'd keep you on if I could."

"Jack, I'm sorry to be blunt, but I don't believe that."

"What?"

"I don't believe you, Jack. I've been demonstrating this product for years. I fill in for you as one of the highest-rated speakers on the circuit. I help troubleshoot customer satisfaction issues, help the development team plan for product advancements, and scope out the opposition to create your marketing playbooks against the competition. Jack, I just don't believe that I'm not talented enough for you to keep me on. I think there's something else you're not telling me. I appreciate the effort of a sugar-coated speech, but I need you to tell me the truth."

"Pete," Jack says. He pauses, either for effect or to give himself time to think. "I underestimated how well you know me. You are indeed very talented. We don't have a spot for you here as our trade show guy. And, as part of the acquisition, we don't have any other spots opening. The new owners have people who do what you do already—they're the largest software company in the world. I'm letting you go, and to be honest, by your request—because it was either you or Tatiana."

The truth sends a chill to my soul.

"And while you're talented, while you bring more money into the business, and could likely replace both her and me in a heartbeat, you don't have a husband in a coma and you don't have to face the prospect of supporting two kids on your own. Hell, I don't even think you have a car payment. And I couldn't sleep at night knowing I've fired a woman in that situation. I may be a heartless son of a bitch at times, but not on this."

"Thank you, Jack. I appreciate the truth."

"You're welcome."

"What's the next step?"

"We're going to pay you two weeks for every year you were here, put you in a placement training program, and let you finish out the week."

"You'll want to keep me through the month. We have a show in Chicago—it's not big, but it might be the most focused and important event we do this fall, considering." I feel obligated to tell him the truth. "Once that's over, send me on my way."

"What's so important about one last event?"

"Momentum. There are several plays in place already, printed items you don't want to explain while trying to spin how great a move it was to be bought. You're going to have too many things on your plate in transition to think about filling this gap."

"Fair enough. After this last show, then."

"Who else knows?"

"Right now, just you and me."

"I want to tell Tatiana."

He looks puzzled. "Okay. That saves me from having to duke it out with her over this. Is there something I should know? It's a little odd you want to tell her."

"Well, Jack, I love Tatiana."

"Really?"

"Yes, I'm in love with her. Why is that surprising?"

"When you came to me five years ago to sell me on this trade show business, you couldn't wait to get out on the road. I'd think if you were in love with her, you'd have wanted to stick around."

"It was complicated; she was married."

"Well boyo, I hate to break it to you, but she's still married. She still has two kids. Why not go after a young girl, a pretty girl, a model with fewer miles on her, not one who's so—I don't know—*plain*." He stands, drink in hand, looking over the window frosting to her office.

I stand next to him and enjoy the view. "I think she's beautiful, Jack. I can't explain why or how I feel; I just know that she's the one I love."

She looks up from her computer and notices that we're watching her. With a crooked smile, she gives a small awkward wave. Jack and I instinctually attempt to duck, but realize it's too late, and give a weak smile and wave in return.

"Well, good luck with that. You're doing me a favor. She'd rip me a new one if I had to tell her you were leaving." He looks like something in his head has finally connected. "Well, that makes sense I guess."

"What's that?"

"She feels the same way about you. Now that I think about it, it makes a lot of sense. There's no one in this office she sticks up for more than you."

"Who are the other people leaving with me?"

"Three people in accounting, the legal team once the thing is closed, and the two sales people with the lowest pipeline this year, once I figure that out."

"Makes sense," I say, moving to the door.

"Peter, do you have any ideas on what you're going to do next?"

"Get you more business from one last show, Jack."

"Knowing what you want out of life is the best gift you can give yourself. I respect you, Peter. You call and let me know if you need a good reference."

Walking to him, I extend my hand for the last handshake with Jack Fowler, 1,004,524.

Gently I tap on the door to get her attention.

"Hey."

"Got a minute?"

"Sure."

I close the door behind me and sit in the chair for guests. All seems right in the world—she's on the side of the desk she belongs on, and I'm just passing through for a quick conversation.

"I was just talking with Jack."

"I saw that."

"He told me the company is being purchased; the announcement's at four o'clock."

"Oh good," she says with a huge gasp of relief. "I couldn't keep that to myself much longer. Not talking to you about everything really sucks."

"I know. I feel the same way."

"What else did Jack tell you?"

"I'm going to be finding another job."

"What?"

"The new company already has someone who runs trade shows; I bet they have a whole team of people who do it. But I'm not going to be part of that team."

"Oh. So you're moving over to sales? Or the product side?"

"I'm going to be moving on to another company."

"He fired you? Peter...." Her eyes begin to well up. "I'll go talk to him. We can find someone else to let go."

"No, this is the right thing. I've had offers from other companies in the last year; I'll find something else."

She's sad. There's little I can do to comfort her here. When she opens the bottom drawer for tissues, I know that the photo of us is there. With a few careful dabs she sops up the tears without spoiling her makeup. The tears continue until she finally stands up. I rise to meet her and she grabs me in a wet and weepy hug.

"I'm so mad at you."

"I know."

"You had to tell me about Yuri."

"I did."

"But you waited to tell me how you feel."

"I know."

"I hate you so much for not telling me."

"I deserve it."

"But somehow you're still alive because of all this. There was something that put all of these things into a sequence of events to keep you alive."

Between the tears, she turns her head and squeezes a little tighter. "We work so well together."

"We did."

"I'm never going to enjoy work this much again."

"You might."

"No, no, I won't."

"You might."

"You're going to take a job that takes you away again."

"I don't know."

"What will you do for money?"

"I have savings."

"How much could you have saved?"

"I haven't spent a dime of my own money in six years."

"You haven't?"

"No. Every paycheck goes into savings; everything else is on my expense account."

"Oh." She looks up. "Well, that makes sense."

"I never spent a dime of my own money. All those frequent flyer miles, hotel points, I have more than I know what to do with."

"What are you going to do next?"

It isn't the question I'm hoping for.

"I'm not sure." I'm hoping for an invitation, a hint that we might spend more time together, or some innuendo of picking up where we left off two months ago, on the couch of that crappy corporate apartment. "I guess I'll start looking for something new."

Chapter 18

I take the train to Chicago with my one carry-on piece of luggage and computer bag. The train's a rare treat for me and takes about the same amount of time as flying from Detroit to Chicago, and without the frisking.

The first gin and tonic warms my belly. After a few minutes the lucid state of easy travel blankets my mind as I settle into my first-class seat. Watching the countryside, I drift back in time to a point when my mother's friend Barb took me with her to the airport. We were picking up her sister, and we walked to the gate to meet her. When Barb's sister came up the runway from the plane, she and Barb embraced at the gate, tears filling their eyes. Around them other couples embraced as well. That can't happen any more.

Now they hardly let you slow down to drop people off outside the terminal. No more teary-eyed goodbyes at the gate between lovers. It's an age of self-sufficiency and rush, security, hostility, and suspicion. Tatiana and I will never be able to share a moment like that.

And in this state, I can't stop myself from remembering the last day I'd been in the office. I was overwrought, and my emotions were triggered by unexpected things. I never want to think about bad things, but my mind seems to dwell on them when I'm under the influence.

In this case, I remember a specific business card I'd kept in my drawer since the very first customer conference Tatiana and I worked on together in San Francisco.

Kevin Yackabowski, Director of Event Sales, The Palace Hotel.

The other day it was just one more scrap of paper to throw out from the bottom drawer of the stupid desk they still kept open for me in the office. When I picked it up, it detonated. I was covered in jealousy and hate for Kevin and Tatiana. I'd suppressed it but it all flooded back.

The two of them had been working on the event for months through conference calls, email, and fax. At one point Tatiana mentioned she was going to fly out for an additional site visit but didn't need me there. Three days before the conference began, when his team had the face-to-face meeting with me and Tatiana, it clicked. I shook his hand, saw the way he looked at her while handing me his card, the way she looked at him in return. All of the pieces fit together; she'd cheated on her husband with someone, and it hadn't been me.

Picking up that business card made me relive that whole week. In an instant I was angry and jealous and filled with hate for Kevin. It had been the reason I'd spent so much time with Tatiana that week. Nothing would happen while I was with her.

In some ways this was the best thing that could have happened since it was the start of my annual relationship with Tatiana. Once a year, I got to spend huge chunks of time with her, squeezed into a single week.

Maybe her infatuation was isolated to only that one San Francisco visit. Maybe nothing at all had happened. But perception is reality. As long as I thought something had happened, it was just as bad as if it actually had.

After checking into the hotel on the Chicago River, I unpack and make my way downstairs. The event's organizers are in the final preparations before registration will open. I look around for Audrey, the top dog. She and her crew are expecting three-hundred-fifty attendees, making it a small and intimate group of experts and peers discussing the most important aspects of their businesses. One of my customers is presenting at the conference. He is one of the top minds on this topic from a systems perspective and I have to keep track of him. I'm hosting a dinner and mixer at the restaurant across the street in a private room for forty-five people. It's busy, but nothing out of the ordinary.

Audrey's assistant, Lindsay, greets me with a hug. She's a few inches shorter than I, with the athletic build and deep tan of a volleyball player. She's intelligent and articulate, with a great smile and winning personality. She's well put together in a smart outfit and her hair is just right. I can see how she's moved up the ladder quickly and holds so much responsibility.

"Peter, how are you? It's so good to see you." She greets me with a hug.

"I'm great, Lindsay. How are you?"

"Doing well. Things are almost done before the big rush for registration. I wanted you to know that everything's ready for the hospitality event tonight."

"That's tonight?"

"Yeah, your company always hosts the first-night event for the conference."

"Oh, I'm sorry. I was thinking of the dinner I have with customers tomorrow."

"Oh, no, this is strictly drinks and appetizers, everyone on their feet."

"Okay, good. I thought I'd missed something."

"Are you okay?"

"Sure, yes, of course. Why do you ask?"

"You look a little discombobulated. It's not like you to mix things up."

"I guess that's true. I could use a break, I guess."

"Okay, now I know something's up. You never need a break. Is it the acquisition?"

"Yeah, must be that. Where's Audrey?"

"You didn't hear?"

"Hear what? I haven't gotten an email from her in months."

"She has cancer."

"Oh my God, that's awful. What kind?"

"Lung cancer. They were treating it with radiation and chemo, but now it's spread to her brain."

"Dear God, that sucks."

"I know."

"No, that really sucks. She's a great lady; I really enjoyed working with her."

"We all do."

"So you've been running the show for a while?"

"Yeah, I was able to head up the team the last few months to get us here."

"What a great opportunity for you. It sucks about Audrey, but she was smart to hire great talent to support her in the tough times."

"Yeah."

Later in the evening, after my hand starts to get sore and after asking one of the sales guys to slow down on the free drinks, I find myself nearly alone in the ballroom. As the last man, I watch the bartenders pack up their wheeled carts with the last of the beer and wine. Melted ice drips, making lines in the carpet as they push. The clacking of stacked chairs follows as a team of men and women set up the room for the next morning's breakfast.

"Peter?"

It's Lindsay doing one final sweep of the room, still looking great, everything in place. My voice is a little weak from the hours of talk about software and business, so she only gets my gentle nod as a hello.

"What are you still doing here? I'd have thought you'd be out with clients."

"Sales guys took them out."

"Are you alright?"

"I don't know."

"Well, that's not a good sign."

"I lost my job with this merger."

"Oh. no."

"This is my last show with them."

"Have you got another job lined up?"

"No, I'm not sure what I want."

"Come on, get up." She offers her hand to me.

"Oh, no, no more drinks for me, please."

"Nope, nothing like that. Trust me."

It's a phrase not uttered to me in years. It's an honest act of kindness I've not received before. She takes my hand and holds it, keeping me close. Her breast brushes against my arm as she leans in, escorting me up the levels of escalators, across the lobby, into the elevators to the 14th floor for the elite members. I'm always highly aware when touching a woman, even in the most casual of circumstances. Do they feel this too? Or are bras so thick they lose some level of sensation? It's my floor and I presume she's walking me to my room, until we turn right instead of left.

After a quick card swipe, she takes my hand again and kicks off her heels. We land on the bed fully clothed and just lie there. She has a long day behind her and two more matching its busyness to follow.

Her bed is heavenly. Mounds of pillows cover the headboard. She edges back to the board to sit up and takes my head and places me in her lap, my cheek to her breast. For a while she strokes my hair and sits silently until our breathing matches one another at a slow and steady pace.

"When we met two years ago I had an instant crush," she tells me.

"You did?"

"But I was in Atlanta, and you were—well—everywhere else. I was always so happy to see you at all of our events, and hoped I'd see you more often, but it wasn't meant to be."

"I think you're great…"

"I know. But you don't feel the same way. There's someone else."

"How did you know?"

"I'm a woman. Intuition."

"Really?"

"No. I asked Audrey about your status. She told me that the first time you came to our conference you were here with a woman you worked with. Tatiana?"

"Yes."

"She said when she saw the two of you together, she just knew. But you never talked about her, Audrey never spoke to her again, she just went on working with you. But she knew."

"Audrey is one smart lady."

"She is. Is Tatiana still in the picture?"

"No, well, it's complicated. It's part of what has me messed up."

"I thought that might be the case. Do you want to tell me about it?"

"I'm not sure. I've never really talked about it to anyone in detail before."

Halfway through the hour of details, we moved over to the couch where I began to rub her feet and to work away the hours of standing at the conference with deep pressure. I talked about the first day Tatiana and I met, the pink top she wore during the interview, that pink bra strap that always seemed to peek out at me during every meeting, the red high heels she always wore with that amazing blue dress, the time we spent each night on the phone, the pictures in her desk, the hurricane hideaway, her husband's coma, the other woman, and the chemical reaction in my mind stirred by the scent of perfume and hand cream. When I told Lindsay how Tatiana had walked out after my telling her of my longstanding celibacy, Lindsay finally spoke up.

"Is that clock still ticking?"

"Clock? It's a calendar."

"You know what I mean."

"Well, yeah, it is."

With that, Lindsay leaned in and started to kiss me. It started on the lips and worked down to that area of the neck just below the ears. Hands, there were hands touching and stroking. Legs began to move and ease into a more comfortable position. Kissing, more and more slow kissing.

Chapter 19

"The first thing you need to understand is that it's not your fault that you're here," the session leader tells our group of twelve. "Let me say that again: It's not your fault. You need to forgive yourself for any hard or mixed emotions that you might have."

His shirt looks as if it hasn't been cleaned or pressed properly. He also looks tired. Not the tiredness one has from having too much fun, but the kind people with a second and third job show. As if there's always something more to be done, another mouth to feed, bill to pay. I have to respect this kind of exhaustion.

"You, sir." He points to me, the friendly face in the crowd. "Why are you here?"

"It was on my schedule," I say.

"And how long have you been out of work?"

I look at my watch. "Four days."

A groan comes from the rest of the group.

"Tourist," says a cynical woman.

"Yeah, try two months," the man to her right says.

"Two months? Try six." A man on the other side scowls.

"Okay." The leader regains control. "We're all at different points in our careers. But we have to remember to be good to ourselves, not beat ourselves up. Next, we need to get organized. Take an assessment of where we are in our lives, our finances, our abilities, our capabilities. Ask yourself, what do you want out of life? What do you want to do? You can do anything. What do you want? Be open to new opportunities, new possibilities."

Driving back to my furnished month-to-month rental apartment in a not-so-great part of town, I attempt to answer these questions, the important ones. What do I want? Tatiana. What do I want to do? Spend the rest of my life loving her. Unfortunately, that position is technically filled at the moment. I'm not sure my current resumé would line up with the qualifications, especially with the recent blemish of Lindsay now on it.

My first task after the morning session is to set up my newly purchased laptop. Today's job seeker, I am told by the man with the poorly pressed shirt, needs to be online. Nearly 95 percent of all jobs come from a pre-existing relationship. Being online, you can leverage those relationships in a quick and easy manner.

My new laptop is small. And fast. Perfect for someone who travels. I made these selections knowing that I do not need a lot of computing power and speed. I need access and portability.

Two hours after pressing the power button, I'm ready to go online. My first stop on the Internet is my email. Empty. Tatiana is working; why would I think she'd write? It's only been three days since we last spoke. But then again, it's been three whole days since we last spoke. Why hasn't she called or written me back?

My next stop on the Internet is a search for professional resumé builders. By only spending a few dollars now, I can easily increase my annual earnings by 3-6 percent, a solid return on my investment. A good resumé and lots of relationships are what you need to be successful and that is what I will have.

This will also be leveraged into an online resumé page. Building a personal web page has become very easy in the last few months. These sites can be tied into a blog for thought leadership or insights into a profession. These are amazing times in technology, and I need to be at the front of where it's going.

My energies rise. My hopes build. My optimism increases. I should have job offers rolling in by the end of the month. Just a few phone calls to a select group of people I'd want to work for and this small bump in the road should be behind me in no time.

Absent all of the parameters of daily operations for business—with all this extra time to focus on me and what I want—my mind starts to open to other possibilities. Do I want another job right now? Yes, if I don't work soon, my skills will be less sharp, as Tatiana explained earlier in the year. What do I want to do? I made this choice to get away from Tatiana, while still remaining in some distant orbit in her universe. Can I be closer? Do I need to be further away? What kind of role do I want to play in an organization? What did I like about the last few years, outside of spending time with Tatiana?

Without much thought, I find the website of my primary airline and look at my frequent flier miles. The number is much larger than I remember. This month's statement of credit card miles, rental car points, and actual miles flown with platinum accelerators has caught up with me and pushed me over a milestone. I've been too distracted with life to think about it. The number itself was never a goal, only a byproduct of what I did.

An alert comes from the laptop, letting me know a new email has arrived. In hopes it's Tatiana I switch over to find it's from the airline.

The email is quick and personal. "Peter – I see you are online right now and wonder if you might have time for a call? I've tried your cell phone in the last week, but think your number has changed from what is listed on our records. Please call me at your earliest convenience at one of the following three numbers below. I'd love to speak with you personally about your recent achievement."

I dial one of the numbers, and the author of the email picks up almost immediately.

"Peter," he says. "Thank you for calling so quickly."

"How...."

"This is your personal number to dial in; I had it routed to me so I could speak with you personally. Congratulations! You have been a busy flier."

"Thank you?"

"I wanted to personally welcome you to our Exclusive Fliers' Club. You're going to be our tenth member."

"Wow, really?"

"Yes, really. I want to deliver a packet of information about this club. What's the best address for you? Do you have plans tomorrow?"

And that's it. With the one phone call, I've become what in industry terms is a "Mega-Mile-Flier." Nothing I had planned for or expected. Just something that had happened. Some of the perks include my own toll-free number directing me to my personal travel agent, a personal valet at any airport, and first-class upgrades for life on every flight.

In the morning, I wake to a persistent knock at the door. I wrestle with my pants and shirt from the day before. Hair messed, teeth feeling fuzzy, eyes barely open, I'm greeted at the door by an airline pilot in a freshly pressed uniform with the name badge "Chuck," standing next to an airline attendant I immediately recognize from the safety video shown on every flight. She's the one with the huge smile, beautiful eyes, and the slight lilt of a southern accent telling me to fly safely.

"Peter?"

"Yes."

"Sorry to wake you so early in the morning, but Sylvie and I are here to deliver this urgent packet to you."

"Would you mind if we came in?"

"Please, yes, sorry. It's not much."

"That's alright honey," Sylvie says with her southern charm. "We're a surprise for you and totally understand."

They follow me into the room and make themselves comfortable. Next they explain that I should clean up and pack for a quick trip to the headquarters in Atlanta. They want to personally introduce me to the team that will be taking care of my travel needs in the future. There will be photos taken, so I should dress appropriately. This will be a day trip, and they'll have me back home that night.

It sounds like a fun distraction. So I do as instructed, leaving them in my "living room" for a good half hour.

"Oh, you clean up very nicely," Sylvie remarks.

It's the best suit I own; most of the others are still at dry cleaners scattered throughout the major cities of North America waiting for the day I'll pick them up. I wonder if I'll ever be able to pick them all up again.

The three of us get into the limousine waiting out front for the drive to Detroit Metropolitan Airport. During the ride it's a challenge not to stare at Sylvie's legs, with their firm long shape under stockings and a skirt that is cut above the knee. She fills the time talking about her adventures in the air. Describing what a real treat it is to have met the first nine Mega-Mile-Fliers and now the tenth. It's been at least two years since the last time they did this and I'm the first after the 9/11 attacks.

Rather than pull up to the front terminal where I normally enter, or the hotel next to it where the smaller and faster security line resides, we drive up to a small gate I've never noticed. Chuck shows a security badge and the gate opens. This takes us to a booth where a bulldog of a man in a navy blue uniform checks each of our photo I.D.s and allows us to proceed. Our destination is the small private jet, engines running, on the tarmac. We pull up and walk on. Very simple and quick.

Inside, the plane is lush and comfortable. Each seat looks like a leather recliner luxurious enough to sleep on during several trips around the globe.

Chuck's not one for talking. He lets Sylvie continue to explain the tricks and tips about the airlines. How her clock for pay starts when the door closes, not when people are boarding. The best seats for people who get motion sickness are over the wings where the ride is smoother. Chuck chimes in to explain that the FAA uses five-letter codes at invisible markers in the sky: His favorite is the approach to Kansas City Airport-"SPICY" and "BARBQ."

We arrive in Atlanta. The flight is much faster than a commercial trip. A car meets us and we take the short hop over to the world headquarters. As I step out of the car I'm greeted by a literal red carpet, flanked on both sides by applauding airline employees. Blood rushes to my cheeks in embarrassment and instinctively I begin to wave in a presidential fashion. My back is now as straight as I can make it and I walk confidently up the carpet to the building. Along the way I see the familiar faces of attendants I've flow with over the years. I stop and give a friendly hug to a woman who seemed to be on every leg of my north-south flights on the west coast. A few more steps and I see the woman who helped me clean a seat that the passenger next to me had spilled on; she deserved a hug as well. Each of the smiling faces belongs people who've been with me in one way or another in the last years to support me. It's at this moment that I realize it wasn't just Kurt in Chicago who helped me to be successful, but there was a whole team behind me.

Reaching the top of the steps, near the building facade, I turn back to see them all still clapping and I give the double-handed wave with a lump in my throat and my heart filled with humility. I might just be the luckiest man alive.

Inside the pristine lobby I find a trio of executives smiling at me. Each shakes my hand.

"I'm Ed." 1,004,632. "This is Dick Anderson, and Terri."

"Thanks for coming down here today," says Dick, 1,004,633.

Terri smiles. "You have an impressive record, Peter. Our first nine were international travelers, while all your miles are domestic." 1,004,634.

Since stepping out of the car door, my time has been filled with constant chirpings from two men with cameras, clicking off dozens of still images with each minute that passes. My well-documented trip from the car up the steps to the lobby is now followed by my historic trip to the top floor via a large elevator. History is then captured of me making my way to a large three-dimensional relief of the airlines logo, where the executive team and I stand with a plaque and they present me with a Mega-Mile-Flier card made from a lightweight and shiny metal. There's also a series of photos as I remove my original membership card from my leather wallet and present it to them in return. My old number and card will be retired and hung with the other nine above this sculpture.

As I sit at a nice lunch with the executives and Tom, Lauren, and Amber, the three people who share the honor of being the Mega-Mile-Flier personal assistant program, our conversation returns to me.

"Peter, what type of business do you do?"

"Well, I was in software for the last few years. I was the manager of a highly aggressive event marketing program."

"You're not now?"

"No. I was let go from my job last week."

The room falls silent at this news. Apparently the bio they've built and shared with the good people in the room includes detailed background on my flight habits, the cities I've been to, my seat and meal preferences, but failed to note employment status.

"I'm sorry to hear that." Terri breaks the silence. "Do you know what you'll do next?"

"I'm not really sure. It's only been a week now. I haven't decided what's next."

Normal noise levels return as others begin to eat and talk with each other. This is the moment I realize that there are two types of people now—those who have somewhere to go and something to do, and those like me, whose schedule allows for a quick day trip to Atlanta.

Terri asks, "What type of expertise did your work require?"

I try to explain as best I can, without too many details, about the planning, networking, contracts, contacts, product knowledge and display that were involved. I also reassure them that several companies in the last year have asked me to consider working for them. I still have hope there's a place in the workforce for me, past the Dot Com bust and the terrorist attacks.

Terri smiles politely and listens to my tale. At one point I'm not certain if I'm informing her or attempting to convince myself that things will be all right. I may still be in denial.

The people at the airline leave me with a warm feeling of appreciation. Amber, a twenty-something blond southern belle, tells me that she's my primary contact. Her business card has an email address and my personal 800 number on it. If I call the number, my call will be forwarded to whomever is on duty among the three, but she's my primary planner.

At the airport, Chuck and I part ways. He's going to "dead-head" back home to Minnesota and Sylvie will take me to Detroit.

Sylvie and I get back on the private jet and find ourselves in flight shortly thereafter.

"Would you like a drink?" Sylvie asks.

"Actually, a gin and tonic would be great if you're offering."

She returns with the drink in hand. After adjusting the seat across from me, she sits and we now face each other. Her smile is that big and friendly smile from the video.

"We didn't know you'd lost your job. We would have been more considerate of that."

"I have nothing on my schedule. Your visit came at the perfect time. It's not like I really lost my job—it's still there, but someone new is doing it."

The joke is old but she still laughs.

"You know, I've had the pleasure of meeting all the Mega-Mile-Fliers. You're the youngest by far. And when I heard that you'd flown all those miles domestically, I must say I was impressed."

I sense a change in her attitude with Chuck absent.

"It came as a surprise to me," I tell her. "It wasn't a goal to hit those numbers; it just happened."

Sylvie looks great in her uniform. I suspect that she's been well aware that I've kept her legs in my line of sight the entire day. Again, she smiles. With a little turbulence for encouragement she leans across the gap between us and begins to kiss me. The chair accommodates both of us as her tiny frame lands in my lap. Our kissing grows deeper and is followed by stroking and caressing. Her large and impressive breasts aren't natural but fun to play with nonetheless. As I work my way up her skirt, she makes a little moaning noise that sounds like a whinny. I quickly discover that the hours on her feet have given strength and power to her legs as they wrap around me and introduce me to the Mile-High Club.

In Detroit she makes her way to the terminal while I go to the car to take me home. She's made my smile as large as hers, I realize. In the last month I've had more sex than in the last six years. Talk about streaks.

This is a good thing, I decide. A break in the Tatiana-centric mindset I have been in for too long. This is my opportunity to move on, if there ever is to be one.

Back in the apartment I call Amber.

"Peter! That was fast. How was your flight home?"

"Good, thank you."

"How can I help you?"

"I have free time. I think I want to take a trip. What can we do?"

Chapter 20

It's morning. As an early and fresh start I'm indulging in a large breakfast. My neck is sore, parts of my back ache, muscles in my legs flicker with tightness, sinews that stretch past my buttocks to my back are alive and dancing. This is the post-sex pain. I need a larger breakfast to fuel my day.

At the bank I withdraw $2,000 from savings and transfer $10,000 into checking. At the electronics store I purchase a power converter pack for all parts of the globe and a high-end digital camera. Back at the apartment I pack three pairs of khaki pants, one pair of jeans, one set of shorts that I can also swim in, three casual shirts, two dress shirts, and enough underwear, socks, and undershirts for five days into my carry-on bag. I'm wearing comfortable shoes, slacks, a collared shirt, and a lightweight neutral- colored blazer. Everything else that is mine in the apartment goes in the trunk of the car.

In the executive airport lounge at DTW I create a blog called "Everywhere Man" off the song made famous by Johnny Cash. My voicemail message to Tatiana is brief. "Hi. I haven't spoken to you in a few days. I was hoping to tell you this in person. I'm not sure how to tell you on voicemail, so I'll be quick and to the point. I'll be gone for the next month or so; I've decided to do some personal travel. I'm not sure if I'll have a phone signal, but I'll be checking my email. I love you, Tatiana, I'm in love with you. I should have told you this in person years ago. And this might be the worst way to say this, but I want you to know. I need you to know. This trip I am taking, it's something I've wanted to do, see the world outside of the exhibit hall. It's something I need to do. I'll call when I land. I'll talk to you soon."

I'm not sure if I say everything I want to say, or even sure exactly what I said, but it's out there now. And I am moving forward down this path of life.

Chapter 21

The call comes right after my private guide cracks open the thin crust of black Pahoehoe volcanic rock. It's heat powerful enough to melt the thin polar fleece I've wrapped around my waist for the pre-dawn adventure. It's hard to imagine that John Hall stood nearly in the same place I'm standing, ready to end it all. It would be difficult to get close enough, let alone make the jump. You'd have to be in a very dark place to overcome the natural reaction to this searing danger.

The name on the display says "Jack Fowler" but I take the call anyway. After that, the guide takes me back through the minefield of lava, its pointed edges and loose bits making it the most difficult hike to rush. Along the way I call Amber and ask her to find the fastest way back to Detroit.

So here I stand, at Tatiana's front door, six weeks after leaving her the first voice mail, and since then, sending her daily emails and dozens of letters and post cards. Fresh snow has covered the old snow; the drive and walks are untouched. Her car has a thick crusty coating of ice that will take a herculean effort to remove. My fresh tan is no match for the air temperature. I knock at the door. I try the door chimes. Finally I try the knob. It's unlocked.

Inside, the air smells foul, like a boy's locker room or a fraternity house on Sunday morning. It's dark and I almost slip on the pile of uncollected mail in the front hall, slick on the marble front entrance. Several of my postcards and all my letters are included in the mess.

To the left the living room is clean. In the back of the house I find the kitchen sink, the source of the smell, full of fetid standing water and dishes black with mold. The fridge holds festering lasagnas, bean dishes, and cold cuts sequestered in plastic containers, each with a little bit of tape or black marker and a name like "The Little's," "Midge," or "Jenkins."

I make my way down the hall to the front of the house and walk up the stairs calling for Tatiana. At the top I find the girls' last Halloween costumes-they'd been a tube of toothpaste and a toothbrush. The picture of the two of them is fresh in my mind, on the steps in front the pumpkins they'd hand-carved, so good looking from the hours their mother had spent sewing their costumes, finding the right lampshade for the top of the toothpaste, taping and painting boxes to fit a little body and finding white bristles to make them both come to life.

The door to the master bedroom's ajar; the shades are drawn, and Tatiana's in bed on her side.

"Hey, I let myself in," I say softly.

All I hear is the whimper of an animal in despair, barely audible, exhausted, and alone. I take off my shoes and crawl into bed with her, wrapping my arms around her slender waist, and wait. I can feel her body rise and fall. I can hear the sound of early morning snow blowers in the distance.

Jack Fowler was clear on the phone. While I'd been gone, things had changed. The week after I was let go from Comp-U-Soft Yuri had finally died after spending that last month off life support. That was why I hadn't gotten a return call, the reason I hadn't gotten a return email from Tatiana. Two weeks after his funeral a drunk driver had hit her mother-in-law and the girls. It was late, the roads were slick, and everyone was exhausted from the months of uncertainty between hospital rooms and missing school. No one survived.

With the fresh snowfall, Tatiana is now in a hibernation of grief, waiting for a new season to begin. I join her for a long sleep. The change of time zones and fast pace of the last six weeks have worn me out. When I awake in this strange place it's dark again. As I get up to find the bathroom or light switch, she speaks for the first time.

"Where are you going?"

In an instant it comes back to me-I'm not lost in the darkness, not in a new hotel or new city. I'm home with Tatiana.

"Bathroom," I say.

I find the light switch and fan. A quick look in the mirror and I can see I'm well-rested and relaxed. I'm done thinking only of myself.

When I crawl back in bed, she takes my arm and wraps it back around her like a seatbelt.

"You snore," she says sadly.

"I know."

We lie in the stillness again. I'm wide-awake, watching the lights dance across the ceiling when a car passes or the neighbors pull into the drive. I can hear her from time to time awaking, sometimes in tears, other times scared. Each time I hold her tight and say that I'm there.

In the morning I awake to a sunny day. As I get out of bed, she's quick to ask, "Where are you going?"

"Bathroom," I say.

After retrieving my carry-on from the car and taking a shower, I put on fresh clothes and decide it's time to tackle the kitchen. Maybe it's the clacking plates going in the dishwasher, or the rotten food I'm removing from the fridge, but something wakes her in a terrible rage.

"What are you doing?"

"Cleaning."

"No."

"Sorry?"

"Who do you think you are, coming in here? This is my house! You're in my house! What the fuck, Peter? Why are you touching everything? Stop!"

"Whoa, whoa, I was trying to…"

She cuts me off. "I know what you're trying to do. You have no place here. Get out! Get out!"

I attempt again to explain my sincere efforts, but she'll have nothing to do with it. She's shrill, irrational, malicious, and begins to take full swings at me.

"I hate you!"

"I know."

"I really hate you. Just when I needed you most, you're gone. You tell me things and run away. I open myself and you're not there. I hate you!" She finally gets in a good pop to my face.

"I know." It all seems so familiar.

Then I remember. There was a point, a moment in time that I knew this rage and madness. As a teenager, a year after my mother's death, I was this angry. It took a doughy large man, Pastor Bill, to grab me and pin me down. Nearly sitting on top of me, he said in an exhausted voice, "Embrace the sadness, then move on." It struck home with me. There was no escaping that I was going to feel exactly what I was going to feel.

So I go to her. I take the rolling pin from her hand forcefully, embrace her squirming body as she tries to get away, and softly begin to say in her ear, "Embrace the sadness, then move on." By the seventh time I say it, her screams of hatred pass, attempts to get away stop, and she begins to cry. When I loosen my straitjacket grip, it becomes a hug, and she embraces me back.

"I'm not going anywhere. I'm here to stay," I reassure her.

We stand, locked to each other, for some time until finally she says that she wants to go back to bed. So I take her back upstairs and tuck her in. Her hair's greasy and lumped in tangles. Her skin's oily and blemished. She's been wearing her tattered old black AC/DC t-shirt and tights like a uniform for god knows how long. My only thought is how beautiful she looks. How I could still smell that amazing scent she carried from the first day we met. "This must be what love is," I think.

Oh, how I wish I'd known her when she was young. I'd only seen pictures of the time when she was much cooler, still smoked, listened to music that would have made her parents angry, and done things just for the experience. But the young version of me would not have had a chance with the young Tatiana-she was out of his league. She still is. Yuri was the right guy for the young girl who stole this tee-shirt at a concert. Yuri was the right blend of daring bad boy with a dash of stability from the strict Russian home his mother had shaped him in.

She looks up to me from the bed with a sadness in her eyes that might never go away.

"You stay here for a bit," I say. "I'm going to clean things, not change them. In a little while, I'll come back to get you. I have a plan; it just needs a little work. Do you trust me?"

"Yes."

Chapter 22

I move the sofa into the kitchen. I take the big television from the family room and run the cable into the kitchen. I take blankets from each of the girl's rooms and put them on the sofa with pillows and make a little fort for her. A little nest where she can watch me move around the house and hear me in every room. It's steps away from a clean bathroom, right by the food she's neglected to eat for weeks, and full of distractions by way of the TV screen.

When I help her downstairs, she sees what I've been up to and settles into her space without a question or complaint. She's catlike in her ability to sit in the sun for hours, just watching what I've started to call "The Peter Show." Today on The Peter Show, Peter learns how to wash dishes. Next, on The Peter Show, Peter practices making peanut butter and jelly sandwiches. On a very special episode of The Peter Show, Peter learns the importance of not mixing chlorine products with ammonia-based products.

I am not very domestic. For many years people have vacuumed for me, picked up after me, washed for me, and delivered meals to me. It's now time to make up for all those years.

Tatiana needs the encouragement of specific questions or else she'll remain silent. I begin to call her "Honey." "Honey," I say. "On today's episode of The Peter Show, Peter needs to learn how to clean a bathroom. Can you tell Peter how to do that?" She calls out step-by-step instructions followed by a "Now remember to...." "Remember to get the grout;" "remember to pick up objects when you dust;" or "remember the floor is not what you are aiming for."

It's good to hear her talk. My childlike understanding of how to live gives her someone to mother from time to time. I can almost hear a tinge of happiness in her telling me what to do. She finds all this entertaining.

It's the second week of our new routine of The Peter Show. From her nest on the sofa she gives me step-by-step instructions on making coffee, cooking food, where items should be put away.

I try to protect her. I jump to change the channel in the first few seconds of the commercials that make her cry. Advertisers play on her emotions with kids in cars, running through fields, things with big red bows, puppies. Just as I think things are getting better, they turn. I embrace the sadness, and move on to the next thing. I am not leaving.

The mail is finally sorted. There are unpaid bills. There are postcards I've sent, letters I've written; some are still to arrive. There are many cards of condolence.

There are strong and enduring women throughout history who have faced similar circumstances. Jackie Kennedy had family and staff and support to become Jackie Kennedy Onassis. Tatiana doesn't have that family or support. But she has me. She needs time and care and attention. Fortunately, these are all things I can give her.

On today's episode of The Peter Show, Peter learns to pay bills. It takes three hours to call all the utilities while she is asleep upstairs. I've paid them and they are now all up to date. Midge, whose Tupperware is now clean, stops in, noticing lights and movement. She sends her teenage son over to clear the walk and cars. I give him the last of my cash on hand for the good work. I call the local grocer and ask if they take credit cards and can deliver an order, which gives us new rations for the coming week's episode of The Peter Show.

"Yes", I tell them. "We will need that many boxes of tissues," and "Yes, that's the right amount of toilet paper."

In our third week, Tatiana begins to talk on her own, without the aid of The Peter Show. It starts with, "Do you have pictures from your trip?"

"I do. Would you like to see them?"

She nods yes and I retrieve my laptop with the thousands of photos. I plug it into the television and she curls up with me on the sofa. Scrolling through the photos I tell her about the people, the places, and the activities. When we get to certain points, I pull out the corresponding postcard or letter if it's available. When I realize she's fallen asleep, I stop and go about my day. When she asks for more, I start where we left off.

Every relationship comes with conditions. My goal is simple. Make an environment where Tatiana can feel safe. Still, at times, I can feel myself waning from the efforts. This is about her. There are things in me I feel changing. Spending this much time with one person can alter how you feel about them.

On the trade show floor you meet all types of people. My counterpart at a credit card company, who did fewer events than I did, once told me that to keep his mind occupied he played a little game called "Binary Love." With each woman he saw or met, he would ask the simple question, Would you ever have sex with this person?

As a kid, my friends and I played a similar game, but we always posed hypothetical conditions. Would you have sex with the most beautiful woman in the world if she were missing teeth? Could you do it with a supermodel who smelled really bad? As the game went along, the questions became more grotesque. What if she were missing an arm? Or missing a leg? Would you if she had no limbs, just stumps?

However, with me and Tatiana, with this game of Binary Love, there are no hypotheticals. No matter the best case or worst case, would I still have sex with this woman? Yes. The real question is, would she ever have sex with me? No matter what I do for her, will she ever love me in return? Could she?

"Tell me a story from your trip."

"I was part of a tour group in Segovia, Spain to see the Roman Aqueduct that's still standing from the First Century. People in tours often travel in groups or twosomes. They're part of a family, or paired with someone else to see sights. Usually it's easy to identify them by the second or third stop. Those four are a family, the mom, the dad, the kids. Those two are on a honeymoon. These two are retired and seeing the world. But there was one couple on the tour I just couldn't figure out."

"What was it?"

"Well, the two women were far apart in age. Mother and daughter? But they didn't look anything alike. Was the younger one adopted? They were always arguing, or putting each other down. The older one had gone through some extensive plastic surgery."

"Really?"

"Yeah, her eyebrows seemed a little higher, or she was always surprised. Her ears were kind of-I don't know- distant from the rest of her face."

"Oh."

"And when I sat closer or stood next to her you could see the pretty fresh scars."

"Yikes."

"So I made friends with the other person who was by himself on the tour. We decided to have lunch with the two of them during our scheduled stop. They served these suckling roasted pigs, which tasted great, but looked, well, a little too like what they were for the women. My new friend and I were able to figure out through casual conversation that they were not a couple, as he'd thought, but were aunt and niece."

"Oh, I wouldn't have guessed that."

"The aunt had gone through some "procedures" in California a month earlier, and the niece had recently graduated from nursing school. The two had been traveling through Europe for the last four weeks as the aunt recovered."

"That's a nice way to recover."

"Yeah, I guess. The two had spent too much time together and were bickering about everything."

"It's funny how people treat one another."

"How do you mean?"

"We've been together for about the same amount of time, but we've only had the one fall out. I think I may even like you more after all this time."

"It's easy being with you, Tatiana."

She leans in and kisses me tenderly. "Thank you."

"You're welcome." I stroke her hair.

On this week's episode of The Peter Show, we welcome a very special guest. Benjamin Waterman III Esq. would like to see Tatiana, in person. He's over six feet with thinning hair and dressed in a well-tailored suit. I ask him to wait at the door and check in with the nest to see if she can move to the living room, if she's up for a conversation. To my surprise, she's ready.

Our meeting in the living room is the first time I've spent any time there. Waterman is polite, but specific in his explanation. Yuri's airbag had not deployed. Statements in the police report caused further investigation. These investigations led back to the manufacturer of the airbags and the company that had assembled the vehicle. While there was no way they could bring back her husband, they would like to offer this check under the condition of Tatiana's signing this document.

The check is substantial. More than I imagined it would be after a description like this. Before Tatiana can answer, I step in.

"You know, in a matter like this, we'd want to consult our lawyer first."

Benjamin Waterman III Esq. does not look happy. "And your relationship to Tatiana is?"

"He's a family friend," she answers.

While the "friend" description cuts me, I continue with, "And we would want to consult the other occupant in the vehicle who witnessed the ordeal, and whose airbag did deploy."

"You know Tammy Lynn?" Waterman asks.

"Yes. Would you like me to invite her to the next meeting, with our lawyer present?"

Waterman smiles and leans over to pull out a second folder that looks nearly identical to the first. This folder has a red label on it rather than blue, and includes a check twice the size of the first. "My clients are very interested in your cooperation in this matter."

"Could you please give us a moment?" Tatiana and I excuse ourselves to the kitchen.

In hushed tones Tatiana begins, "Why the fuck do you have Tammy Lynn's number?"

"I don't. I just said that to see what his reaction would be."

"What should we do?"

"You should take the money. I don't think you're interested in sitting in a courtroom or spending years with a lawyer on this."

"But this could be just a small portion of the money; there could be a lot more behind this in a settlement."

"Is money that important here? This check is a lot of money. Do you really need more than this? Even taking off the government's cut, it's still a lot of money."

"What could we do with this?"

"It's your money. What do you want to do?"

"It's mine?" She sounded almost puzzled.

"Honey, I love you very much. I hope you know that. I would not still be here if I didn't. But this is your money. You could set up a fund in the girls' names, donate it to a worthy cause, or save it and decide sometime in the future what it could be used for. I don't think you'll forget how you came by this money. The older we get, the more I realize how short life is. You don't want to spend it in litigation."

"You're right. I want to live," she whispered. Then she shouted, "Benjamin Waterman III Esq., do you have a pen?"

Chapter 23

In marketing, the importance of networking cannot be over-emphasized. Trade shows are a great way to meet a large number of new prospects. Post-purchase interviews with independent research firms confirm that trade shows are one of the top three tactics organizations use when conducting early due diligence in product assessment and product knowledge. Here we are—two parties, one with a solution and one with a need—let's get together in large groups and meet on a topic.

Networking also includes connecting prospects to the right people in your organization. My organization is now made up of Tatiana and me. Which is why our first stop on the way to John Hall's wedding is Las Vegas.

We have had more progress in the last few months. Money does not change things for the better, but it allows you more freedom to make choices. Tatiana wanted to put the past behind her and sell the house. The things, she decided, were just things. They were not her loving daughters or her unfaithful husband. Sometimes she still cries or wakes up scared; she's human, it's normal. We are moving on. You can't hate yourself for the things that you've done, or the things that have happened in your life. You have to love yourself for surviving and having accomplished what you've accomplished.

The conversation in which I told Tatiana about Lindsay and Sylvie was unpleasant. In perspective, those were not good choices. But I felt the need to be honest with Tatiana. I had always told her everything, and there was no reason to start hiding anything from her now. She understood. She was not happy, but she understood. I guess your own regrets are not always as hideous as you think. As for Kevin Yackabowski, my new policy is not to ask questions I don't want the answers to.

Tatiana and I sit at the bar of the Star Trek Experience. It's a slow night and I introduce her to my friend Phil the Ferengi.

"Ah," he says, looking at me slyly. "Hu-mon love is very valuable. And you know that Ferengi always seek things of great value." Tatiana glances at me and laughs.

"No," I promise her. "This Ferengi has true wisdom."

Phil tells Tatiana the tale of hu-mons in Greek literature. How they were eight-limbed balls of flesh rolling through the world at great speed until they tried to rise against the gods. Once struck apart, they became empty and alone, seeking to fill their voids with one another. And when they found their other half, their former match, they knew in an instant.

"So, they just fit together?" Tatiana asks.

"Tatiana." I smile now, sure of the answer. "The greatest thing you'll ever learn in life is just to love and be loved in return."

She leans against me and I put my arm around her and hold her tight.

"Hu-mons," Phil says, shaking his head dismissively. "Easier for a Ferengi to love a good car wash."

But I know better. No longer am I a satellite in orbit around Tatiana's world, but around her heart. During late nights I am not a concern on her mind but her consort in life. We are intertwined for the ages, rolling at inconceivable speed across the universe. Hers is the best handshake ever.

About the Author

Paul Michael Peters is an American fiction writer based out of Ann Arbor Michigan. After studying at the Second City in Chicago he spent extended periods of time living in Philadelphia and Toronto before returning home to his beloved big mitten shaped state. "Peter in Flight" is his debut work.

You can follow him online at www.paulmichaelpeters.com where he posts a blog called "Everywhere Man".

CPSIA information can be obtained at www.ICGtesting.com
Printed in the USA
LVOW04s0023030915

452555LV00030B/1466/P

9 780989 178518